Book of Never

The Phoenix of Kiymako

Ashley Capes

The Phoenix of Kiymako
(Book of Never: 6)
Copyright © 2018 by Ashley Capes

Cover: Illustration by Lin Hsiang, Design by Vivid Covers
Layout & Typeset: Close-Up Books

ISBN-978-0-6482600-4-2

www.ashleycapes.com

Published by Close-Up Books
Melbourne, Australia

For Never fans everywhere!

Prologue

The creature is dead.

It cost the Empress twenty-three of her finest men but it is done. Pieces of his body are scattered not just within the Imperial Cemetery, but beyond it too. I myself dumped a hunk of the thing's torso in the ocean, though it turned my stomach to touch even the wrappings.

I mark these details now, here in my own journal, so that knowledge of its death is not lost. Empress Feyania wanted no official record of the man – or beast, if the truth were known – and while I agree with much of her reasoning, I must acquiescence to my fear, and act against her decree with these words.

We have done our utmost to ensure it does not rise again, but should such a dread event reoccur, let these warnings ring true: do not believe that one arrow or lunge will kill such a man. He took over a dozen of each before he fell – and prior to this, we had already managed to burn his wings to ground him. Even then, he continued his destruction for his very blood can suck the life from a man or sear flesh from bone. The creature continued to burn us until my Lieutenant severed the man's head.

Only then did it stop.

It is a miracle that we cornered the creature in the first place. But he did have a weakness; his appetites for flesh were well known – if Sergeant Trapelo hadn't tracked it from the brothel to the ruin we would have lost its trail once more. Among many regrets is that I cannot properly honour Trapelo's work today, nor bring comfort to his widow.

Still, I will write this now and entrust the words to my successors.

Pacela, My Lady, please spare your golden land from another Thing such as he – if not forever, at least in my lifetime.

Hodenva
Captain of the First Imperial Guard
Signed in the Reign of the Empress Feyania of Marlosa

Chapter 1

"You're stalling, Never. It's obvious."

Elina lay in the undergrowth beside him, peering between the bright green fronds of bracken toward the shaded road. Her dark hair had been pulled back from her face, tied up to prevent an enemy getting a hand-hold. The role of Princess seemed to agree with her; there was a contentedness that he hadn't seen the last time they'd met – though a flicker of annoyance was clear too. Their mark was late – no surprise, truly; the gross tardiness of the common thief was all too predictable.

"Of course I am," Never said with a frown. "But I think I'm being subtle enough." The scent of damp earth was strong, almost welcome after the harsh sun of the clearings.

"Is that so? It's been three days since you arrived," she replied. A smudge of dirt grazed her pale cheek. "Shouldn't you have booked passage by now?"

"Keep this up and I'll make it three more."

She raised an eye-brow. "You don't have to wait for Ferne, you know. There must be half a dozen other river boats heading west you could use."

Never opened his mouth to reply but the crack of a whip stopped him. The rumbling of carriage wheels drew near, still muffled by the dense birch, but the rogue nobleman was finally approaching. "Ready?"

Elina nodded.

"Be careful," Never said, then stood to leap and catch an overhanging branch. The bark was smooth beneath his palm as he swung himself up, then climbed higher. He stopped at a vantage point that offered clear line of sight to the tree that they'd felled across the road.

An obvious ploy but it would work – someone always had to get out and remove it, no-one ever turned back. And more, it'd give Never and Elina a chance to see just how many men Baronet Fabiam had along on his treasonous little jaunt into the forest.

As a dark mare drew into sight, cresting the small hill, Never leaned forward. "Hope your driver's watching where he's going for your sake," he said.

A sturdy carriage followed the horse and the driver had just enough time to jerk on the reigns to prevent sending himself, his mount and carriage smashing into the fallen trunk. The mare whinnied in protest as she skidded to a halt.

The fellow was cursing from the platform as the carriage door swung open. A guard wearing the livery of the Baronet climbed free, a hand on his hilt as he surveyed the trees. The driver was calling back to the man.

"Tree on the road."

The guard barely glanced at it; instead he continued to focus on the trees. "It could be an ambush. Get the axe."

"Sir." The driver hauled himself down the steps and ran

around to the rear of the carriage.

A bowstring snapped.

The guard gave a shout, falling to the ground. He clutched his knee where a feathered shaft protruded. Elina was already stalking forward, pale blue cloak stirring, a second arrow set to string.

"Throw your blade aside," she ordered the guard.

Never rolled his shoulders, letting his wings free but keeping them close to his body, waiting, ready. One heartbeat. Two. He fell, wings spreading with a snap as he swooped down to thump onto the carriage roof.

A yelp came from within, but he drew a knife and pounced upon the driver. Never swung hard, striking the man across the head with the pommel. The fellow collapsed with a groan – there was a chance he'd survive at least. Never hadn't meant to swing quite so hard but it was best to be sure.

He charged around to the door.

Within, a fop in a yellow and black livery complete with a small, peaked hat, was cringing against the opposite door. He fumbled with the handle, his eyes wide. Never reached in, grabbed a handful of cloth and hauled.

The Baronet crashed to the road, a puff of dust following. Then he gaped up at Never's wings.

"Stay," Never growled.

The man flinched.

Elina was already approaching, her expression rather unforgiving. The guard was bound, his weapons beyond reach. Blood ran from the swordsman's knee and Never ignored the way his own blood stirred at the crimson. He positioned himself between the man and Elina, allowing a clear view of both the guard and Fabiam.

"Where is it?" Elina demanded.

The man lifted a trembling hand to point at the carriage, all without taking his eyes from Never's wings. Never flared them as wide as possible, black feathers filling the edge of his vision.

Elina ducked into the carriage, rummaged around a moment, then returned with a head-sized wooden box. From within she drew forth a bronze disc marred by patina, a clump of straw falling away. The bronze design within was a stylised image of a man rowing a boat, possibly beneath the sun or moon. Never gave a low whistle – he'd seen enough antiquities to know something truly old when he saw it. Old and valuable. Nothing that would have helped him with his old quest; it didn't appear Amouni, but it was still impressive. Perhaps dating back to Sarann's heyday, before the city was buried.

Nobleman Fabiam was certainly going rogue in style.

Elina set it on the ground then drew a knife, pointing it at Fabiam. "Who are you selling this to? Answer quickly."

"Jorga. He's Vadiyem."

Elina glanced over at Never. Trouble or coincidence? Vadiya involvement could be entirely incidental. It was too soon after the aborted invasion.

"He buys Hanik artefacts?"

"Yes. That's all, Lady Elina."

"Not a brilliant idea there, Fabiam," Never said. "Couldn't you find anyone else to sell to *other* than the country that just invaded your own? Maybe he's selling more than artefacts. The charges of treason just keep mounting, don't they, My Lady?" he said to Elina.

Elina nodded. "Indeed they do."

Fabiam rose to his knees, hands pressed together. "Please, I stole the Solar Disc and the other pieces but that's all it is. Jorga only wants trade to re-open between our nations and to have a head start when it does. And I only did it because I need the money."

"What do you think, Never?" Elina asked, her expression unimpressed.

Never checked on the guard, who still sat bound, face white with pain, before shrugging. "I think he's hiding something – maybe I could take him up for a little flight? We can see how high he bounces when I drop him."

Fabiam froze, his face draining of colour. "My Lady!"

"Interesting idea, Never," she said.

"We can bet on the outcome; it doesn't even have to be height. How about number of bounces?"

She pursed her lips. "First, why don't you clear the road for us."

"My pleasure."

Never drew one of his knives, the pattern of interlocking triangles raised against his skin. He made two quick incisions in his palms, deftly avoiding old scars. Blood welled and heat with it as the ancient Amouni magic stirred within him. Globes of flame grew, engulfing his hands in the crimson-fire.

Fabiam shrieked.

He ignored the man, instead flinging his hands at the huge tree trunk. Twin streams of blood shot forth and seared through the wood. Smoke rose from where he cut each line, working quickly. When a large, central section of the trunk thumped free, Never gave it another blast, sending the hunk rolling clear.

"There." Never turned back to offer a quick bow.

Elina was grinning, though Fabiam was crumpled in a heap and the guard's eyes were wide, his mouth agape. "Beautiful, Never. But before we load these traitors into the carriage I'd like you to make sure that piece doesn't start a forest fire, if you don't mind."

Chapter 2

The Baronet had broken rather quickly.

Perhaps it was the dark and grime of the dungeon, the threat of plummeting to the earth, seeing the crimson-fire or Elina's repressed anger, but Fabiam didn't seem to have anything worse to answer for than greed. Elina was still going to chase down Jorga, of course, but it didn't have the feel of anything larger.

"I doubt the Vadiya have the resources or the heart so soon after withdrawing," Never said from the deep armchair he'd sprawled across. Elina was pacing before her fire, its heat not unwelcome. She stopped to lean against the mantle, toying with a dagger hilt.

"Retribution doesn't have to come in the form of another attack, Never."

"Assassination?"

"Why not?" she said. "We were both involved in driving them out."

"Then how do they get messages in and out? That bronze disc wasn't hollow."

"It could be both; we're searching the carriage and the other men. And remember, this isn't the first thing he's stolen."

Never shifted, flipping a leg over the other arm. "True. But I still don't know. Fabiam seems rather undermanned for another rebellion or assassination plot."

"Let's wait for my men to return before we call the Baronet undermanned."

As if summoned, a knock came on the door. Elina barely answered before it swung open, revealing an old man dressed in the head steward's green-striped robe. He was breathing hard, but his expression of concern eased when he saw Elina.

"My Lady, you gave us all a fright," he said, his papery voice revealing a deep weariness. "Please, you mustn't be so headstrong anymore. You are too important to the Kingdom."

"Deyllid, everything is well, as you can see."

"This time, yes, but you have a personal guard for a reason. We all want you safe and they want a chance to perform their duty. They train most diligently," he added.

"Very cruel, Deyllid," Never said. "Guilt is a dangerous emotion to bandy about like that."

"Good evening, Lord Never," the man said.

Elina sighed. "Deyllid, it was entirely by chance that we stumbled across Fabiam; there wasn't time. But I promise, I'll bring the men along next time."

He gave a short bow. "My concern is for you firstly. And I know it might seem almost trivial, but I worry about everyone, especially after the manner in which your predecessor operated."

Elina crossed the room to put a hand on his shoulder. "And I appreciate it. Without you to remind me, I fear much of the good work that happens here would go unacknowledged."

The steward bowed again, it seemed from Never's position in the chair, to conceal his smile of gratitude. "There is also the matter of the treasury meeting, Lady Elina," he said when he rose. "It will be exhaustive."

Now Elina smiled. "And so I'd best get some sleep is what you're saying, I presume?"

"Trying not to say, Your Highness. It would be untoward of someone of my station to presume to do so."

"Well, good advice is good advice," Elina said as she thanked him. The steward excused himself and then Elina was back to pacing before the flames.

"You don't seem very tired," Never said.

"I can't make a mistake. What if it's something bigger than it seems?"

"Then you'll find it and stop it."

"I appreciate the confidence," she said but her tone expressed doubt. "But I don't know, Never. There's so much to attend to and even though Grandfather and Deyllid help, it's my responsibility. I didn't ask for this but if I'm going to lead my nation I want to do it properly."

"Like this treasury meeting?"

"Rebuilding isn't cheap, and the money has to come from somewhere." She shook her head. "I can't worry about that now. I want to be sure of Fabiam."

Never stood and stretched. It had been wonderful to fly again, even briefly, but he was feeling a little couped up in the chair. And even if Elina wasn't tired he couldn't deny a sluggishness to his own limbs. "Then let him free with some sort of degrading punishment, then watch him. See if he meets with this Jorga again; that way you'll catch any conspirators," Never said as he approached with a frown. "You *are* tired; you wouldn't usually need me to work this out for you."

Her shoulders slumped a little. "Perhaps you're right."

"*Perhaps?* I should be insulted; when have I ever been wrong?"

"Plenty of times. Never..." She paused then, meeting his eyes a moment before looking away once more. There'd been something vulnerable there and perhaps only the second time he'd ever seen such a look on her... but it was subtly different to when she'd told the story of her brother's death. And now she was waiting, as if gathering strength to speak again... and when she met his eyes once more, she was smiling. "Thank you for today. Why don't we both get some rest."

"Ah, good idea." He hesitated a moment then started across the room. At the doorway, he looked over his shoulder. Elina was already gone, the door to the adjoining chamber clicking shut.

In the hall he strode past tranquil paintings and the gleaming silver in the windows until he reached the guest wing. There, he kicked off his boots and lay back on the soft bed. What had Elina wanted to say? And her smile when she thanked him... had it held a trace of sadness? No, regret.

Regret?

Never sat up.

"I am a damn fool."

Something stopped her, but Elina had been going to ask him to stay... hadn't she? He lay back down and shook his head. No. It had been something else, surely. And in the end, she'd chosen not to speak whatever had been on her mind.

Never frowned up into the darkness of the room.

By dawn, he'd not come any closer to clarity and when a servant knocked on the door to inform him that Captain Ferne had arrived, Never began to pack his belongings. Whatever Elina had decided, she'd decided last night. Stopping in City-Sedrin had always been part of his plan to reach Kiymako. Take the River Rinsa west and then travel the ocean north toward the giant island, where hopefully he'd find evidence of his father, and more importantly, his sister.

If she still lived.

And *if* she truly existed in the first place.

All he had was his brother's certainty – not that Snow had often been wrong. There was the vision too; the one Never had received after drinking the vial mixed with dust from his father's ground bones. Was it all a little thin? Well, he'd searched after thinner rumours.

Even as he walked through the quiet halls, heading for the exit, he shook his head. It was a strange kind of lie he told – it changed to suit him. In the forest, Elina had told him he was stalling and it had been true, for what if he reached Kiymako and found nothing? No trace, no clue to follow.

Or worse, if he found clues and they led to naught.

Losing the last thread of family...

Yet after last night, he was once more on the trail like a bloodhound, confidence creeping back despite how little he had to go on. "It's just that Ferne's finally arrived," he muttered to himself.

And even that seemed like a lie.

Sacha's words echoed in his head like a sharp answer.
Running away – what you always think about.

But hadn't the showdown with Snow broken him of that pattern? Wasn't that the reason he hoped to check on Luis and Tsolde if he could, why he'd stopped in City-Sedrin in the first place? Never came to a halt, starting down a corridor that would take him back toward Elina's rooms.

But when he arrived, a servant handed him a folded piece of paper and explained that the Princess was already meeting with her council and could not be disturbed. Never thanked the girl and started back down the hallway, his boots echoing in the morning hush. The palace was still mostly abed.

Once out of sight, he stopped to open the paper.

Never,
I know you will find your sister, do not give up.
And don't get yourself killed!
Elina

Quite brief. And no mention of last night.

Relief replaced a flicker of disappointment. Elina was beautiful and strong, exactly the kind of woman he desired but she was a friend. They'd been through enough together, knew each other well enough now... maybe that was why she'd said nothing? Perhaps he was imagining things in any event. Vain fool!

He smiled as he tucked the paper into an inner pocket and started back toward the great entryway. Elina would be fine; she had a nation to rebuild, a still-recovering grandfather to care for, and a bold but non-treasonous thief to deal with. She'd forget last night soon enough.

As he had to, if he wanted to find his sister.

Never checked on his purse, the reassuring clink of coins following. Now, all he had to do was make sure Ferne didn't try and fleece him. If the big man was as rich as he'd planned to become, surely the captain wouldn't need to charge too much for what should be an uneventful trip?

Chapter 3

Ferne's fortunes may have changed but he hadn't – he still wore a bear-like beard of black, his head was still bald, and he certainly hadn't lost his broad axe. Admittedly, the former treasure-hunter now wore a much finer cut of cloth, a maroon and black tunic and earrings of gold that caught the rising sun, the first warm spring morning.

"Never." Ferne started down the gangway of his ship, speaking over a din from the docks; a mixture of sea-birds and grunts and cursing from the men loading and unloading goods. "I got your message."

"Did you think I'd be dead?"

"Ha, you're too clever for that. I just didn't think you'd need to book passage on one of my tubs, is all. Aren't you the Winged Hero of the war? I hear about you in every damn port. You're twelve feet tall and your wings are like a cloak of midnight, you've got fire for blood and no blade dares touch you – and that's only the half-believable stuff."

"And so legends begin, I fear."

Ferne slapped him on the back with a large hand. "Well,

I can believe most of it – except the stories about your wings. I admit, that seems too much, even for someone like you."

"Well, I'm not planning on flying all the way to Kiymako."

"That's what I thought." He gestured to the ship, a sleek hull painted a deep blue, its oars drawn in and the mainsail still. Barefooted sailors worked at various tasks, one coiling a dark net, another climbing down a rope ladder to check the hull for barnacles. "The *Swordfish*. Much smaller but faster than my other ships."

"Looks good to me," Never said as he followed the captain across the gangway. "How many do you have now?"

"Six," Ferne said. "Since our little expedition to the Amber Isle, the wind has turned in my favour."

Never lowered his voice. "The Sea King's Eye?"

He nodded. "Hasn't led me astray once; no storm, no channel, no reef has been able to surprise us. It's an infallible, glowing compass from the very Gods. I've even managed to sail around the Southern Horn and if you think there were a lot of wrecks at the Amber Isle, well, the horn puts the isle to shame."

"How does it work on a river?"

"Not as wondrous but I'm not expecting trouble on a simple passage, am I?" he asked, and it wasn't really a question.

"I won't if you don't."

Ferne showed him to a tiny room not too far from his own quarters. "We're not exactly a passenger ship, but it's all yours."

"More than enough, thank you."

"We'll be travelling directly to the Stone Bell, where we can resupply. The Rinsa's Curve will get us to the lowlands where we can travel west again. The old Rinsa slows a bit where it widens down there, but there's no way to carry the *Swordfish* up The Long Stair so that's my best offer."

"I trust your navigation, Captain."

He snorted. "Navigation? It's the largest river in all of Hanik, nothing to navigate."

"Still, better your hand at the tiller."

"Don't worry, you'll do your share – cooking and hunting at the least."

"A chance to stretch my legs, perfect."

"Once we reach the coast it's only two days to Kiymako." He paused to frown. "I hope you've got an idea for permission to dock. Word is that they've tightened trade even further thanks to the Vadiyem. Supposedly only captains with existing contracts are allowed to enter the bay now – newcomers, even those with spice, are turned away with burning arrows."

Never raised an eyebrow. His last, rather brief visit to Kiymako had been after something of a shipwreck. He'd landed to the north of the island and while no-one had been precisely welcoming nor were they as disagreeable as Ferne was suggesting. "Excessive."

"No ships sunk yet, but the message spread quick enough."

"Well, I do have a plan and I promise the *Swordfish* won't face a single arrow."

"Good. Get settled; you can tell me about the war when we're underway," he said as he left.

Never unpacked what little he'd brought. Much of it was mundane travel items for cooking or camp, but several possessions he hadn't let out of his sight since Snow's death. The Amouni robe was packed at the bottom, not that he'd ever need to use it again, a single bloodied white feather, and the item he was most concerned about – the golden seed from the Memory Tree.

He'd not tried to see within but neither had he shattered it... nor could he decide whether his reluctance was folly or prudence. The potentially far more dangerous *Hor Pyrilh*, the book Snow had called the Human Map, was still locked up in Pacela's Temple.

Once Never had unpacked, he headed back above decks where he moved to the prow, doing his best to keep out from underfoot. He glanced up at the silver city until the work was done and the *Swordfish* was sliding down the river. Hard to shake a twinge of regret... or was it lingering confusion?

"Never?"

One of Ferne's sailors stood before him; an older man with a salt-and-pepper beard. He was loading up a pipe with black tobacco.

"I am."

"Ferne said we're heading to Kiymako and he thought I might be able to help."

"You've been there?"

He nodded. "Many times; used to travel on a spice merchant. Even learnt the language. I'm Hanael, the ship's cook."

"So you've spent a lot of time there then?"

"I suppose so." Hanael produced a second pipe from his vest and offered it.

"Thank you but I don't care much for it."

The sailor grinned. "Picked the habit up over there, actually – only whatever they smoke wasn't for me. Made me hear strange things."

"Hear?"

"Right. It's hard to explain, if you're a gambling man, try some *yikho* if you can get it."

"If – Ferne mentioned the harbour was closed?"

"Not when I left but that was some time ago, to be honest. They're a cautious type, the Kiymako. Slow to accept outsiders." Hanael sat on a nearby barrel, pipe in hand. "I hear you know the captain from his treasure-hunting days."

"True."

"Said you were different to anyone else he'd met, crafty too."

"Faint praise but it's quite welcome nonetheless," Never said with a grin.

Hanael chuckled. "I only ask because I think you could help me as much as I you."

"Depends what you're asking, I suppose."

"How about this – I teach you what I know, teach you the language, and you retrieve something for me."

"Such as?"

"A ring with a small ruby. No King's ransom, and it's more the value I've given it, if you know what I mean? Once belonged to my wife; I lost her to illness years back now." The man's face seemed to contain no trace of duplicity.

"I see. And how did you lose it?"

Hanael cleared his throat. "Gambled on a sure thing – only I think my opponent cheated me. I made a bit of a scene, you see and now I'm not exactly welcome in Najin; that's the harbour town."

Never nodded. "And the current owner of your wife's ring?"

"Isansho Shika. She sort of runs Najin."

"No small matter, then."

"I'll do my best to make it worth your while, especially if you're a fast learner. Have you speaking Kiyma in no time."

Never rubbed at his jaw. "I'll do my best – which is pretty good, to be honest, but I'm not promising a miracle."

"No-one else is likely to help me."

"Then we've got a deal, Hanael," Never said. "How about the first lesson over breakfast?"

Chapter 4

The banks slid by in an endless flow of dark water, verdant grass and beyond, pale birch forest competing with green. Days blended into one another as they approached the low lands, and the journey doubtless would have been a little tedious without Hanael's lessons, since Never didn't have to row or even plot a course. Thankfully, and as he'd hoped, Hanael was indeed fluent in Kiyma. The language had a kind of cutting rhythm and yet the words were longer; at first the changes to his breathing, had left him a little short of air, but as he'd suspected, he *did* learn quickly.

Amouni blood was still the gift that wasn't going to run short, it seemed. Whatever aptitude for the ancient language the Leschnilef had unlocked was now extending quite nicely to modern languages. Once the patterns became clear, and the rules around the correct sounds, he was confident he'd be speaking well-enough by the end of the voyage, which was still some weeks away.

"How goes it, men?" Ferne asked as he approached one evening, his big beard preceding him.

Hanael shook his head in awed disbelief. "You weren't joking when you said Never was different – I've never met anyone that learns as quick as he does."

"So you keep saying," Ferne said. He gestured ahead, where the river widened even further. "Stone Bell isn't far, thought we'd take a night on land in their inn."

"Still a man of the earth, eh, Captain?" Never asked.

Now Ferne frowned. "Nothing wrong with solid ground once in a while. You pay for your own meal and room."

"Gladly. And you can tell me more about the Eye."

"Only if you keep your mouth shut about it afterwards."

"On my honour."

Ferne grinned. "Didn't think you had any left."

"Plenty to go around," Never said. "I trust the inn serves more than fish?"

"Used to." Ferne glanced ahead. "We'll find out soon enough."

Stone Bell's four-storey wood and stone inn slid into view, windows aglow in the fading light. The *Swordfish* docked at the sturdy piers, quite large compared to the smaller fishing boats, and most of the crew disembarked to pile into the inn, which even with the locals too, clearly had not reached its limit; it had enough tables for twenty more men.

"So, how will you find her?" Ferne asked after the serving girl brought their drinks.

"Go to the first temple I can and ask about a girl with Marlosi heritage. I suspect my father left her in one and it seems unlikely such a thing has happened often in Kiymako. If one temple harbours – or has harboured her – I'm betting the others will be aware of it."

Hanael nodded. "The monks have the best communication

between temples I've seen anywhere. I've got no proof, but I always suspected magic or even divine assistance. If one temple knows about something, they all do," he said. "The first and biggest problem as I see it, would be getting any of them to admit it. Foreigners are generally not permitted to serve the temples."

"But it's possible?"

"I never heard of it in Najin but maybe in one of the bigger cities like Takbisu or Mondami. I wouldn't want to offer false hope."

Doubtless Father had found a way to pressure the monks to take his daughter in; he hadn't drawn a protection-symbol for nothing. "What about the monks themselves?" Never asked. "How many of the rumours do I need to discount?"

"Well, firstly, they aren't *all* warrior-monks, though there are enough."

"And their so-called Temple magic, is that something to worry about?"

Hanael grimaced. "Perhaps. Despite all my time there, I can't say I ever saw it. Apparently only the most devout can perform such a feat. It's called the *lunai*, and supposedly grants great power."

"I'll wager half the *Swordfish* that *lunai* nonsense is just a myth," Ferne said as he drained his cup.

"Like the Sea God's Jewels?" Never said.

He grunted. "I still don't buy it… but from what Hanael has told me you'll have more trouble with ordinary folk. They won't want to help you much."

"Because I'm a foreigner?"

Hanael shrugged. "More that you haven't proven yourself as valuable to the people. There's also a long tradition of placing the needs of Kiymako folk before outsiders, in fact, it's considered very poor form to do so and it's grown stronger over the last decade."

Never frowned. "But on your last ship, you obviously spent a lot of time with the people. It sounds as though I'll barely be tolerated now."

"Maybe that's true enough. But for us, we were bringing much-coveted goods. Cinnamon in particular is highly-prized. When the *Black Rock* sailed I found that if there was ever a time when an outsider's needs had to be weighed against a local, we sailors rarely came out on top."

"I should have brought some cinnamon."

Ferne nodded. "Pick some up at Furnam before we leave."

"A grand idea, Captain," Hanael said. "That might cover Never's second biggest problem."

One of the serving girls arrived with a tray of steaming potatoes and pork sausage.

"Such as?" Never asked around a mouthful of sausage.

"We've talked about it a little already," Hanael said. "Remember the phrases for travel, directions and distances?"

"Most of them."

"Even with that fair accent of yours you might not get far. Without a pass, you won't be allowed to leave Najin and passes tend only to be given to a few merchants. And with the current situation, they might not work even if you get one."

"I'm quite nimble, you know," Never said.

Hanael chuckled. "Good, because I'm counting on your ability to get around unseen, but a pass might make it easier to visit the temples – there's one in every single town and often between them, on roadsides."

"Hmmm."

"You two can figure out the rest without me," Ferne said as he stood. "The *Swordfish* is leaving at dawn and I need my beauty sleep."

"Think just one night's enough, Captain?" Never asked with a grin.

Ferne slapped Never on the back as he passed. "Hard to say; I might wake up and find I've turned into a fairy."

"So long as you can still get me to Kiymako."

"You've paid your way, I'll get you there," he said. "Then it's up to you to figure out how we get into the harbour without being burned to the waterline."

"I've got that under control, Ferne."

"Good," he said, his voice nearly lost in the din as he started toward the stairs. "Tell me all about it tomorrow."

Chapter 5

The *Swordfish* seemed to groan its way free of Furnam's docks, as if laden by the new provisions taken on, including Never's cinnamon, but the ship was soon picking up speed as the Lower Rinsa rushed toward the mouth of the Hanik Straights. The oars had been drawn in and the sail boomed as the ocean neared – a glittering blast of blue water and reflected sunlight stretching to the horizon's bounds.

According to Ferne and the Eye, it would be smooth sailing to Kiymako, a voyage of no more than two days, after which Ferne would continue east to deliver goods he'd taken on, the prized cinnamon among them.

And for several days Never had managed to offer the former treasure-hunter only vague hints about his plan, yet now that they'd reached the ocean Ferne had come to the end of his patience as he stomped over to stand beside Never at the rail.

"Before we go too far north, I'd like to hear how you're going to protect the *Swordfish*, Never. The whole plan."

"If you promise not to laugh, I'll tell you exactly what I

have in mind for protecting your ship."

"Have you ever heard me laugh, Never?"

"Not that I recall."

"Well, do I seem in a cheerful mood now?"

Now Never chuckled.

"So, speak up."

"All right, Captain. Ready? The *Swordfish* is not going to be fired upon because it's not going to get near enough for that to happen. Once land is in sight, I'll handle the rest."

"I'm not wasting a longboat on you, if that's what you're thinking."

"No. I was thinking I'd fly the rest of the way."

Ferne opened his mouth to speak but stopped then he folded his arms. "You're right, Never. That's not funny. You expect me to believe those rumours from the war?"

"I'd rather not startle everyone aboard but if you doubt me, I can show you – I just need some more room, my cabin's a little cramped."

"Never, if this is—"

"It's no jest. I mean to fly the rest of the way; I won't need a longboat or anything else, just a share of the spices we agreed upon. You saw some pretty unbelievable things with me in the Amber Isle – is one more impossibility really so hard to accept?"

"It shouldn't be," he said with a sigh as he stared out across the waves. "And for now, I'll take you at your word."

"Good."

Ferne straightened, leaning forward a little. Then he turned and shouted up to the crow's nest. "Ship sighted, south and east."

The woman spun her eyeglass around and after a moment

called back down. "Vadiya colours. Looks like a patrol ship... it's sailing into the wind, Captain."

"Watch it, Silvya."

"Yes, Captain."

Vadiya's coastline wasn't too much further south, so it wasn't unreasonable to assume the ship was on a routine patrol. A niggling twinge of doubt lingered however, even as the tiny shape began to recede. Was there some other reason for the ship's appearance in Hanik waters?

Yet he had to place the concern aside; it was groundless.

And as he'd told Elina, so soon after the war, the Vadiya weren't going to be looking to expand again. There was a slim chance it was Fabiam's merchant, but in all likelihood it was a patrol only.

By nightfall Never had managed to spend more time on the Kiymako language, and plan a little more of his path once he landed on the enormous island. According to Hanael there were a handful of fishing villages east of Najin where he could probably barter for information. Then, he needed to find the nearest temple or monk to organise a pass – which would probably mean travelling in to Najin anyway, if he could convince them, via his wares, to help.

The other option was to travel alone, sneaking his way into every city.

"It wouldn't be too difficult to pass the walls," Hanael said. "They're wooden, formidable but not unscaleable; it's more once you're within. You'll stand out. Monks will expect to see a pass and if they don't, you'll be imprisoned."

"I might have to do some sneaking then, which would suit me for a time at least, especially if I'm to retrieve your wife's ring."

"Then let me tell you a little more about Najin and Shika."

"The Isansho, the Overlord?"

"Yes. But that's not quite the correct translation – she does command, but it's to overlook or watch over. Each region has an Isansho answering directly to the Divine Throne..." he paused with a shrug. "But there's time for that later. What do you need to know? And in Kiyma, this time."

"Anything about her as a person could be useful," Never said, switching languages. "Her routine, guards, likely location of the items she's stolen – not things a foreign sailor would know, I imagine, even one who gambles with overseers."

"True enough. It was my Captain that got me to that table, but I am sure she still has Mara's ring; Lady Shika thinks of herself as a collector. That's why she accepted my bet; she knew it had value to me."

"So you've said. Anything else?" Never asked.

"The people of Najin consider her to be firm and just, but cold. She's a warrior but I've never seen her without a pair of monks at her side; they're fast. I *have* seen one catch an arrow with his hand."

Never raised an eyebrow. "Really?"

"And I wasn't drinking that night."

"Her routine?"

"There I'm no help, but there's a yearly gambling championship in Najin she hosts, and it's open to anyone who can pass her requirements... but it's not until midsummer."

"Well, maybe I need to focus on her dwelling. Did this championship happen within her walls?"

He nodded. "In a courtyard before the main buildings of the Isansho's mansion."

"I don't suppose they let you wander around?"

"No. But the gates open each night to admit the Gathering Monk."

"Gathering Monk?" There was no special need to use any such gate, since he could simply fly into the compound, but anything he could learn might be useful.

Hanael slapped his stomach. "Right. But, how about I go and see if the lads left anything in the pot first?"

"A grand idea."

When Hanael returned with two deep bowls of stew they found a spot on deck beneath a lantern, the cool night air carrying the scent of salt with it. It wasn't until they'd finished half the meal before he continued.

"Remember I said the temples were important to daily life?"

"Yes. That regular people communicate with them almost daily, but you didn't say why."

"Well, it's probably easier for you to see it in action than have me butcher the explanation. Think of it as a religious and a civic act."

"The people are informing on each other?"

"Not precisely, Never. Like I said, you need to experience it to understand properly – but the reason I'm mentioning it is because the Gathering Monk leaves the mansion to collect important information from the other monks, which he passes on to Shika."

"Like me."

"Right. A foreigner running around with or without a pass would be very noteworthy."

Never took another big mouthful of stew. "Perhaps I'll be blessed with an invite then?"

"Might be in chains."

"Or maybe I'll borrow the Gathering Monk's robes and see how far I get."

Hanael dropped his spoon into his bowl with a sigh of satisfaction. "That'd get you killed, my friend."

"Well, I've still got a bit of time to come up with something."

"Not much if we're going to expand your vocabulary – it's all still pretty formal."

"You said I was a fast learner."

"Then get ready for a few sprints, Never."

Chapter 6

Kiymako's green coastline was shrouded in a low-lying morning mist, but the deep green and blue of mountains reared beyond, visible at a squint as the rising sun climbed slowly. The new light gleamed on fins in the water too, as several sharks approached the *Swordfish*.

Never's pulse quickened a little, not due to the sharks, but simply looking at the coast – his pack seemed lighter than it was and his wings ached, eager to be set free of his body, not to mention the slices he'd made in his clothing. And hopefully his wings wouldn't snag on the straps of his pack either; since plummeting into the sea wasn't really part of his plan.

Once he reached land, if the Gods deigned to be kind to him once more, he'd find his sister and maybe another piece of his past.

And maybe there he'd also find a sibling untwisted by bitterness and delusion.

And just maybe, she'd need him too.

"Ferne, this is probably close enough," Never called back

to the helm. "No need to have you spotted by Kiymako cutters."

The captain crossed the decks. "Still trying to pass off that story about flying, then?"

"Well, I'm not jumping in to play with our friends in the water." He put a hand on the man's shoulder. "Thanks for a safe voyage." For Hanael he switched to Kiymako. "I'll do my best."

"I'll be in your debt."

Ferne stopped him. "Wait, how are you planning to return?"

"I'll get word to you somehow." Never strode to the mainmast and climbed the rope ladder until he was just beneath the nest. Ferne's lookout, Silvya, was sweeping her eyeglass across Kiymako.

"Hope I don't block your view," Never said.

The woman gave a grunt.

Never turned his body so he was facing the open water then stretched his arms up above his head, twisting his torso a few times before letting his wings snap free. A single black feather fluttered away, a hint of purple revealed when the light hit it.

Then he bent his legs and launched himself into the air.

Silvya gave a shout as the mainmast rocked, but Never didn't bother checking on the lookout; the mast wasn't so weak that the sailor would fall. Instead, Never beat his wings, climbing into the sky. Beneath, faint cries of shock followed him up. He glanced down; men were pointing and calling to one another, Ferne and Hanael amongst them.

A gust of wind buffeted him and he banked, letting it carry him across and higher. He took his time, gaining height, even though it meant circling a little, until he would be able to glide some of the way down to the shore.

The air rushed across his face, a welcome sensation – as was the freedom of flight itself. His wings had been restricted so long now...

Ahead, the shape of Kiymako became clearer.

The island was enormous – even from his vantage point he could not see the opposite side, it was more of an entire nation, a landmass not so different to Hanik or Marlosa. Mountains rose beyond the green forests that lined the shore, three in particular caught his eye – like the prongs of a crown.

To the west there stood a giant lake, glittering blue, and beneath it to the southeast, much closer to the shoreline, waited the horseshoe of Najin Bay, and climbing above it in turn, the harbour town, pale buildings a mere smudge. Yet he angled away from it, hopefully toward one of the fishing villages Hanael had mentioned.

Land drew near as his wings began to tire. Never dipped his flight, swinging down toward a cluster of buildings near the shore, their rooves thatched with reeds, or so it seemed – he wasn't close enough to tell for sure, or, hopefully, be noticed. He spread his wings and lifted his legs, slowing rapidly as he neared the earth. He thumped down onto a trail that ran beside the ocean.

Not a bad landing overall, but he'd had smoother.

The road ran east and west. Behind him, the grey and green of a bamboo forest smothered the still-rising sun. The path ran within, straight and broad. Before him, the plant-life grew thinner. Several times the road split into tracks that reached the sandy earth before the water's edge; a dark mass of split reef where the waves broke.

Never took a few steps forward before muttering a curse; his wings. He drew them into his body with some effort, the Amouni magic doing its job, and let his cloak settle over his pack before resuming his trek.

Few sounds competed with his footfalls so early in the day, a twitch in the long grass or the lap of water against stone, sliding across sand, but he still turned at every one. If he ran into a villager or fisherman, he'd probably be able to talk his way into getting help but stumbling across a monk so soon might be more difficult.

And finding his sister meant keeping a level head.

The sun had risen fully by the time he reached the outskirts of a village – the splash of water and hushed voices from around a bend in the trail causing him to slow. He slipped into the thickening bamboo and crept forward, placing each boot carefully. The carpet of leaves was a motley of green and yellow; quite lovely so long as it didn't give him away.

Three men with black hair stood in calf-deep water, bent forward as they talked, words indistinct.

Each wore a pale tunic cinched with a belt, and had their pant legs rolled up. They stood a little apart, all carrying the same equipment – a long dagger and a reed basket. The nearest fellow leant closer to the water and raised his knife, then waited.

The other men fell silent.

A faint popping sound followed and the man with the raised blade swung sharply. As he did, he brought his basket close, as if catching something. He gave a grunt of satisfaction and one of the other men offered a little cheer.

What had he caught?

"You'll be done before noon at this rate," the third said – or so Never thought; the words were as Hanael had taught Never but the distance didn't help.

Never moved away, giving them a wide berth.

As he neared the buildings he'd marked from the sky, he had to bypass two more groups of men – some older, some younger, but all seeming to fish the same way. There were canoes and smaller boats beyond the reefs, too, and those folks seemed to be after actual fish.

A single building – almost a hut – stood at the edge of the village, which spread around an open square with a stone statue of a bird that may or may not have been a phoenix? The buildings were similar in construction, reed thatching and bamboo walls, sometimes chinked with sandy mud.

A few women were out, one hanging white tunics on lines strung between homes, and an older woman with iron-grey hair sat cross-legged before her home, dressed in a pink robe. She was running a whetstone across a long blade with a single edge – a Kiymako tyrant, as they were called everywhere else. Hanael had called it something else... a *sisan*. More blades of varying sizes were arranged before her on a piece of cloth she'd unrolled.

He hailed her softly as he approached. "Good morning. I hope I'm not interrupting you?"

She frowned up at him, squinting a moment, but did not seem perturbed when she marked him as an outsider. "Well you are, stranger. But since you look lost, I suppose I can help."

"Thank you," he said with what he hoped was a charming smile. "I'm looking for the nearest temple."

"You'd want to head to Najin then; it's about a day's walk."

He nodded. "Or perhaps the village has a monk?"

She lowered the whetstone to point beyond the homes, into the bamboo. "You can find old Hiruso in there. He'll be on the *rya* trail, looking for flowers."

"Thanks again."

Never strode between the homes, smiling at a child playing in the window as he passed, then found the *rya* trail. It wound within the shade, leading him between stands and through gentle depressions, and once circling a clear pond. As its name suggested, flowers lined the path, each one a tiny riot of orange petals. He bent beside one; half of the *rya* flower had been sliced free. A sweet, heavy scent washed over him. Faintly pleasant and quite calming too. What did they use it for?

He stood, moving deeper along the trail until he saw a figure crouched ahead.

At the sound of Never's approach, the monk stood.

The man was short and wiry-looking, the hem of his deep-green robe covered in dirt and leaves. Small pouches hung from a paler green belt and his hood had been pushed back, revealing a smiling face lined by wrinkles – a little like the Bleak Man. But the Kiymako monk still had his hair, it was white and threaded with silver beads.

"Greetings," the monk said. "You seem far from home, young man."

"I am," Never said. He hesitated. So far, folk had been more welcoming than he'd expected from what Hanael warned him. How much to reveal about his search? "I was hoping you could help me; I'm looking for a temple."

"Foreigners, even those bearing Grace of the Temple, are generally not permitted within."

"I see."

A voice called from the trail behind Never. "Brother Hiruso? Are you near?"

The monk raised his voice. "Here, Yota."

"Good, because..." A lad caught between the age of boy and man had been jogging forward but now he slowed. He was dressed much like the fisherman – if that's what they'd been – Never had seen before, but the lad carried no basket, only a bright blade at his belt. "Oh. I didn't know you were speaking with another." He went to one knee, then turned to leave. "I'll return soon."

"No, Yota, it is fine. I'm sure this traveller will not mind."

"Please."

The lad shot Never a wary glance before approaching the monk, where he went to one knee again. He presented his knife. "Udasi blessed me with this today, Brother Hiruso. I wish to formally acknowledge his kindness in helping me."

"I am Her Witness to Udasi's generosity of spirit."

Yota stood. "Thank you, teacher."

Then he started back along the trail, once more looking to Never with an expression of doubt.

"He worries needlessly; that much I sense about you," Hiruso said. He was kneeling beside the trail, a pair of scissors in hand as he harvested some of the *rya*.

"That was an odd confession, Brother Hiruso."

"Ah, you must be quite new to our land."

"My first time witnessing such an exchange."

He smiled as he looked up at Never. "And you were told that everyone is constantly spying on one another, running to the monks to spread gossip."

"Not in so many words. That seemed more like an

expression of gratitude."

"Yes. That is our way; acknowledging such goodwill is the responsibility of the receiver. Arranged otherwise and the giver will become prideful." He sighed. "Still, Yota's fear tends to control him. He is even now sending word to Najin about you."

Never frowned. How much time did that give him? "Suspicious lad, and I thought, part of your own role."

"Certainly he has reason, stranger. You appear with little to suggest the guise of a merchant, in a time when so few outsiders may set foot upon Kiymako, in a time when so very few remain."

"I won't be here long enough to trouble Yota or any he calls for." Hiruso did not appear particularly warlike, yet it was always a mistake to underestimate. But if there was a chance Never could learn more he had to take it.

Hiruso nodded. "Without a Grace, without permission, travel will be difficult."

"You said I am not one to worry over and I will say it aloud, my purpose is not nefarious. I'm only searching for someone; a Marlosi girl who would have been reared in a temple – most likely a city."

The old monk did not answer at first, instead returning to his work a moment. Was he holding back? If Hanael had been right about the way the monks shared information, surely even a village monk like Hiruso would have some knowledge. "No such child has existed in Kiymako. It is forbidden."

"I'm surprised to learn that it is not against your teachings to lie, Brother Hiruso."

"No pass exists here, stranger. Travel to Najin by the

Sundered Road and seek the ka-temple by the western gate."

Never hesitated... the man clearly knew more but was pushing now the right choice? Just because Yota presumably couldn't collect half a dozen warriors quickly, didn't mean he wouldn't soon return with a dozen suspicious villagers armed with tyrants. And if Never was being completely honest with himself, he was simply too tired to have to escape with his wings so soon after his flight.

"Thank you, Hiruso."

Chapter 7

He'd found the Sundered Road easily enough after skirting the fishing village, and while he hadn't seen evidence of Yota and angry villagers, he had to assume a search was underway. So he strode into the darkened path despite the misgivings it gave him.

Compared to the proper road he'd bypassed, the parallel path was a thin whisper between bigger, older bamboo and a carpet of ferns. Many of the trunks he passed bore carved markings – the Kiymako language, though he could not read a word of it. Warnings or idle graffiti?

By noon the sun was barely penetrating the canopy; though he could see well enough and a dim and uneven trail was still better than a smooth road crawling with warrior monks. The jittering cry of some manner of bird had fallen away too, giving the forest a stillness that suggested his passage was the only one.

He passed the ruin of a wagon, bamboo growing between the spokes of a wheel and moss consuming the greying sides, and a little further on, a series of rusted swords driven into the earth in a circle that encapsulated the entire path.

Odd. And just why was it called the Sundered Road?

A little further and the answer became clear; gaping holes in the earth swallowed up the trail, the ferns and the bamboo, letting patches of light fall through. The first few holes weren't too large but as he detoured them, it became clear the openings were getting larger. Bamboo grew from some, clinging to the sides, but most holes seemed black pits without hope of return should he fall.

The further he travelled the Sundered Road, testing the earth as he moved, the larger the holes became, stretching far and wide. Light continued to fall through in blazing columns or wide streaks where the canopy had stretched out and over the craters, eventually coming to illuminate a chasm not unlike a small lake. He guessed that detouring to either side would add considerable time to any journey and even delay a traveller enough to prevent them reaching Najin by nightfall – unless that traveller had wings, of course.

Brother Hiruso had seemed sincere, as though he wanted to help. So why suggest such a place? Certainly it took Never out of the way of any hunting party but it was not a path for the casual traveller. Unless the man knew... Never shook his head. "No." *That* was ridiculous. How could Hiruso know about Never's Amouni heritage? The old monk was simply suggesting a path few Kiymako, warrior monks or otherwise, would use.

Wasn't he?

The man's refusal to reveal all he knew lingered and Never turned to face his back trail. If he hurried, he'd make it back to the village before dark, maybe get some proper answers from the man... and walk directly into the arms of whatever warriors Yota had summoned.

Never had to laugh. "Well played, old man."

Hiruso had forced Never's hand; there was no choice. It was probably safer to leave the forest before nightfall, and it was doubtless easiest to sneak across the city and find the minor temple by the west gate during darkness.

"Fine." Never let his wings unfurl and launched into the air, beating hard to haul himself and the extra weight of his pack off the ground. He gained height as he crossed the chasm—

Something snapped around his foot.

Never gave a cry of shock as it dragged him down.

He struggled in the darkness, beating his wings but it was hopeless. Whatever held him was stronger – he scrambled for a knife, slashing at whatever had encircled his boot. The blade hit flesh, hot blood spraying forth, but he was not released.

Down and down it dragged him, the light above growing smaller, no matter how hard he beat his wings.

Never kicked then slashed with his knife once more but still could not break free.

But he jerked to a sudden halt. His joints groaned and a moment later he struck stone, biting his tongue and bruising his hip. It hadn't been a long fall, the final part of his descent, he was well-enough to roll quickly, knife ready, but there was only darkness confronting him.

"Aaaaamouni," a rasping voice whispered. "Yesss, yesss, yesss."

The second word echoed, as though Never stood in a large chamber. He spun, straining to hear over his hard breathing. Yet only the hiss of the 's' continued. Never growled; enough darkness! He flipped his dagger into his palm and sliced into the back of his hand this time, before switching the knife to repeat the cut. Blood tricked forth and he fed his anger into it, letting two globes of crimson fire bloom.

"Don't let any of that blood go to wasssste, now."

A red glow lit his surroundings.

Not powerful enough to illuminate everything, but the shape of branches... or bones, littered the uneven floor. The voice had come from directly before Never; he strode forward, boots crunching over smaller or older bones. Definitely bones.

When he neared the wall, he slowed.

Something clung to it, resting above him at the limits of the light. It was man-shaped... only it had more arms and legs than was natural and a long, tendril-like tail swung in and out of the light. Its end bore several gashes. The head twisted around to regard Never; face obscured but two eyes glowed, reflecting the crimson-fire.

It scuttled down the wall a little, still out of reach, but as it moved Never caught sight of dangling legs, unused. Still attached to the torso, they were withered and pale. Another limb looked like an arm – only now it was skeletal, several fingers missing. Yet the rest of its body, the other limbs were solid, muscular, even the tail, which the creature held poised, not unlike a scorpion.

Never couldn't prevent a shudder – what by the Gods was the thing?

"Long time ssssince an Amouni set foot on the island. I could sssssmell your blood at once," it said, voice echoing. Its mouth and cheeks were covered in a dark stain. Old blood? Mud? Something else? It ducked back into the deeper shadow. "Asssscended too. Didn't think you'd visit."

"You didn't give me much choice."

A snuffling followed – was it laughing? It shifted sideways, moving from the light.

Never tracked it, keeping it within at least the edge of the crimson-fire's glow. "But I'm offering you a choice."

"Oh?"

"I'm flying out of your little hole and you can either watch me do so, or be dead."

The thing paused. "Well, it pays to be ssssure – your wingssss must be whole, unbroken, yessss? It doesn't do well with broken things."

Never flared the globes of burning blood and the creature hissed at him. Then it slipped from the light. Never spun, but the rock face remained empty. His pulse had doubled, and he was breathing hard again – it wanted his wings?

He spun again, flaring hard and caught a glimpse of its leathery tail, heading up.

Never gave ground with a curse. His fire made him an easy target yet with the amount of limbs it had, he didn't like his chances if it came down to knives. "Fine." He flung his arm forth and a stream of crimson-fire shot out to sear into the stone wall. Debris followed, clattering to the cavern floor, but he'd missed.

Again Never spun. The filthy thing could be any – something crashed into his back. The blow knocked him to the floor. A jagged piece of bone sliced into his side, pain spreading with the flow of blood. He ground his teeth as he reached one knee, flinging both arms around his head, spraying thin lines of crimson-fire across the room.

Hissing followed.

He stood. "You come too close and I'll melt you down to the bone."

"Soundssss like you'll need a lot of blood."

The voice echoed still, making it hard to pinpoint the creature. Never guessed, striding forward. Yet when he raised his hands, spreading the light, there were only the stone walls.

Something cracked into the back of his head.

He stumbled forward, vision blurred. The crimson-fire flickered, but he leapt to the side, flaring it again. A grunt echoed and he roared back at it, voice turning hoarse. His every other step now had him scrambling for purchase as his boots found a mass of bone, rising up like a hill.

It was toying with him.

Perhaps its plan was to weaken him; it was afraid of the crimson-fire. But the fire was the very thing that would finish Never if he let it, it was simply impossible to keep up the streams indefinitely.

Yet there was a way.

An old way, if he wanted to risk it.

Never let the crimson-fire blink out. In the inky silence that followed, he closed his eyes and let his blood guide him. Faintly, oh so faintly, it yearned left. He took a step, the pulling sensation grew stronger.

Blood sought blood.

On the way down, Never had cut the creature's tail.

And now his blood sought out a living body to drain. Never released his inhibitions, the rigid checks he usually placed on his curse, his fear of hurting others, and let his blood quest in the dark.

He followed it away from the bones, quickening his steps.

A shriek echoed from above.

The creature scrambled over up and away, limbs slapping against the stone in a frantic rhythm. When it stopped, a grinding of stone followed and then a dull boom. Had it gone then? Never exhaled. He'd driven it away but maybe only momentarily.

Time to fly.

He spread his wings and leapt up, wincing at the pain in his side. Once he'd put some distance between he and the crater, he'd have to attend to the cut. For now, his only concern was escape as he pumped his wings, clawing his way toward the light.

When he finally broke free, Never kept flying until he'd reached the top of the sturdiest looking bamboo tree. He caught it, wrapping one leg and one arm around it, and frowned down at the huge crater and the other openings as he tried to catch his breath and rest his wings.

He'd scared it off, but it was crafty enough to lie in wait near the surface of a different opening. The thing doubtless had access to more than one crater, best to fly quite high, or maybe from tree to tree. Supposedly, it had tasted Amouni blood before – it knew enough to fear the blood, knew about Ascension, yet it also had a clever tactic. Drag an Amouni into the dark, making sure not to break the wings, then force the Amouni to use crimson-fire for light.

Then, it was a matter of avoiding the flame long enough for the Amouni to accidently weaken themselves beyond return.

"Clever bastard, aren't you?"

Never clung to the treetop a little longer before setting out once more, leaping forth and gliding toward another tree. As he did, he kept half an eye on the dark openings below, his mind troubled by another thought.

Had Brother Hiruso sent Never to the Sundered Road, assuming he'd fly across the openings in order to avoid the creature, or had the old man sent Never *directly into the creature's path?*

Chapter 8

Najin did not precisely slumber beneath the stars.

Light and music, mostly flute and drums, sprung up from the harbour. It leapt even over the walls to reach Never where he clung to the bamboo once more, marking the path of a sentry on the walls. As Hanael had described, the wooden walls stood high, sturdy but not insurmountable. If Never had been forced to cover the open ground before the walls and scale them, even with his newly bandaged wound, he'd manage. Especially since it was healing quickly; something he'd long-since started to take for granted.

Of course, he'd be flying over the wall instead, but only once he was sure he'd not be spotted.

And once he had an actual destination.

Brother Hiruso's advice was doubtless tainted. And it was needlessly specific, for a ruse. *The ka-temple at the west gate* – why not say 'find a temple'? After all, what did it matter *which* temple when the old monk had always planned for Never to perish on the Sundered Road?

Or perhaps that was simply the spice to the lie, a bit of

specific detail to really sell it.

"Gods, you're a fool," Never told himself. It didn't matter *how* the old goat did it, it mattered *that* it had happened. Sauntering up to the lesser temple on the opposite side of town was not going to happen.

He needed information from people already within Najin, from sailors, merchants or outsiders, if any remained in the harbour.

And that meant inns and taverns, which wouldn't work, since the entire town would be, if not actively watching for him, willing to rush off and tell the nearest monk if he was seen.

Which only left the wharves.

"Time for a little good luck," he said softly, as the nearest sentry dipped from sight.

Never launched himself through the cool night air. It ran across his face and stirred his hair, prickling his skin. At high speeds the wind tended to sting his eyes, but gliding was always a pleasure.

He swung around the walls and swooped down to skim over the placid waves, approaching the docks. Kiymako cutters with their painted hulls and black sails were mostly quiet, portholes dark or decks empty. Other local boats, fishing craft and a larger ship either for passengers or goods were equally unpromising. Yet half a dozen foreign ships were tied off too – only one bore lights in the captain's cabin. It appeared to be Marlosi by the stallion masthead.

Never swept in to land on the rail at the stern, stepping softly down onto the deck.

He circled coils of rope and took a ladder down to the main deck. Empty. Where were the sailors? No-one in the crow's, no-one stationed in the fore watching the warm glow of the small city either. And, oddly enough, little in the way of noise from below.

Maybe the faint snores of sleeping sailors and hushed conversation – so not a night for the drink, either.

He started along the passage, heading for the glow sneaking beneath the door where he raised his voice. "Is the captain home?"

The murmuring ceased, and the scrape of a chair followed. "Who by the Burning Graves Below boards my ship at this hour?" The words were Kiymako, but the Marlosi accent was clear.

The door flung open, revealing a short man in a silken robe, holding a heavy crossbow. His frown was quite deep, though Never caught a flicker of surprise too. "Well?"

"My name's Never, Captain. I'm looking for a friendly ear," he said, raising his hands. "I have spice."

He grunted. "You're a damn fool, breaking curfew on my ship."

"Curfew?"

"That's what this is, isn't it? You're a new hand and you've snuck across from old Pela's ship to ask if I'll run. Well, let me save you some time, I won't. We're all stuck here until the Isansho says we can leave."

"Actually, I have quite a different question. And I'm not a sailor."

The thumping of footsteps appeared as several cabin doors snapped open, revealing sleepy-looking sailors. "Trouble, Captain?" one asked.

The Captain sighed. "Not sure yet. Into my cabin and bring your club, Deze." To Never, he waved a hand as he turned for his room.

Never followed him into a rather utilitarian room lit by candles, soon joined by Deze and a hefty-looking weapon. Never took a chair opposite the Captain, who set his crossbow aside then rummaged amongst the pages of a ledger, before lifting a quill. "I'm Captain Milagra and you're trespassing on the *Lion*, Never, or whatever you call yourself. Explain – and keep in mind, you've got about as long as it takes me to finish here before I have Deze dump you overboard."

"As I said, Captain, I'm not trying to *leave* Kiymako. I want in; I'm looking for someone and I need information. A pass wouldn't hurt either." He set his pack down, rummaging through it to lift a tin canister free, which he set on the table. "I'll pay for the help too."

Captain Milagra's quill paused. "Cinnamon."

"Indeed."

He looked up, a new light in his eyes. "How much?"

"Half. I mean to save a little for unforeseeable situations."

"Half for whatever information you need?" Milagra pondered. "It'll get us off rations for a little while, right, Deze?"

"Right," the man said, smiling.

"And the pass, the Grace of the Temple?"

Milagra shook his head. "If you're caught with a pass that hasn't been assigned to you, you're dead and so am I. You'll have to make do with the information."

"Very well." Hardly ideal, but Never split the spice, changing some of his Melosi coins for the crescent-shaped Kiymako tender at the same time, and sat back. "First question – have you heard of a monk named Hiruso from one of the eastern villages?"

"Last month was our first time in port. A few days in Najin was shut off – can't say we've had much chance to go sightseeing yet." He locked the spice in a desk drawer. "Hope your other questions turn out a little better, friend."

"Let's see," Never said as he leant forward. "Is there anything special about the ka-temple by the west gate?"

The captain shrugged. "Not that I've heard. There's six ka-temples – lesser ones – in Najin and one Divine Temple within the mansion grounds, but they're all the same aside from the grand temple."

"Because of the Gathering Monk?"

"Him, yes. But I mean, not just anyone can visit it."

"And no foreigner sets foot within any temple?"

"None. Though I can't for the life of me think of why you'd want to; it's full of spies and assassins."

Deze cleared his throat. "And the treasure."

"Forget about that," Milagra said. "It's a myth."

"Treasure?" Never asked.

"Supposedly, each temple holds a secret room with a huge opal used to communicate with other temples. They say each one is worth –"

"Deze." The captain shook his head. "There's more than enough money for us without worrying about that."

"I'm looking for some*one*, not some*thing*," Never said. He raised an eyebrow. "Someone who used to be a prisoner of the temple, an outsider. Maybe they still are, it would have been years ago now. Heard any rumours?"

Milagra gave a low whistle. "In Najin?"

"Anywhere in Kiymako."

"No, but I can tell you who might, if such a thing had

ever happened."

"Who?"

"Wanatek – he's something of a rebel."

"He runs with bandits in the forests," Deze added. "Isansho has been after him for years according to the head of the harbour here."

"Rebelling against what?" Never asked.

"I don't understand it myself," the captain admitted. "Something about succession? His son? It never made sense to me but if anyone's willing to spill temple secrets, it'd be him, seeing as he's an ex-monk and all."

Never nodded slowly. Not unpromising at all. "So I'm going to have to wander the forests until I stumble across him?"

"Either that or try the Green Leaf Inn – Isansho's troops have raided it twice since we've been trapped here."

"Many reasons for the lord of a city to do that, Captain. Maybe the inn's selling watered wine."

"First steps might be small, but they must be taken," the man replied with a grin.

"How wonderfully philosophical," Never said as he stood and lifted his pack. "One more question and I think that's enough information for now, thank you both."

"Go ahead."

"Where can I find such verdant lodgings?"

Deze's expression was a little puzzled but the captain snickered. "Northern Cut, between a baker and a peddler of cheap jewellery."

"Northern Cut?"

"Najin's cut into three parts, you'll see when you get there."

"Good, I love a mystery," Never said.

The captain chuckled. "Well, you're welcome to sleep on the deck tonight, just make sure you don't touch anything."

Never thanked him then let Deze lead him up onto the deck where the stars had gone, muted by a creeping cloudbank. There, Never made some show of preparing a space before a row of water barrels, then once Deze was gone and the light winked out in the passage, Never climbed the rigging and leapt into the sky once more.

Time to drop in on the Green Leaf.

Chapter 9

After a fair amount of impolite knocking, the door to the Green Leaf Inn finally jerked open.

"By the Phoenix's Beak I'm going to..." An old woman held up a lantern, casting her features in hard shadow, but the shock on her face was clear when she saw him. She wore a long grey skirt with a half-length blade belted over the top.

"Forgive me but I'm weary after a long journey," Never said, and there wasn't a shred of untruth to his claim. Not only were his movements seemingly stuck at half speed, but his empty stomach was starting to gnaw itself into a giant hole, and on top of that the hole was eating itself too.

The woman muttered a curse – or so Never assumed, since Hanael hadn't gotten 'round to all of them – before she waved Never inside. "Hurry, fool. You'll bring the whole damn street out and then I'll have to answer to Lei-Dahn tomorrow."

Lei-Dahn? The Gathering Monk, or someone else? "Forgive me, I don't want to cause you trouble – at least, no more than I already have."

"We'll see." She appraised him a moment. "I suppose you'll be wanting a bed, then?"

"And a meal if possible?"

She shook her head. "Cold mutton is all I have."

"Wonderful."

"Then let's see your money, Marlosi-man – and it better not be any of those horse-head coins, either."

He produced a handful of the crescent pieces. "One night is enough for now."

She snatched half the coins from his palm, strode to a counter, rummaged around a moment and returned holding a thin steel plate with circular grooves on one side. "Get on upstairs and I'll bring you something, then."

He accepted the key and thanked her before she changed her mind, taking the stairs two at a time in the dim light. At the landing, he paused, lifting the steel plate. Was it a key? And just as important, which door? He approached the first, wincing at a creaking floorboard. There was what seemed to be a corresponding plate within the door, but its pattern was one of squares. Never moved on, the next two doors were waving lines, the third diagonal lines... until finally, at the very end of the hall and around a corner, was the final door – the design on its panel a match.

Fitting his 'key' against the door, Never slid the grooves into place and pushed, seeing as there was no way to turn it.

A soft click followed.

The key fell free and the door swung inward, revealing darkness. He stepped inside and fumbled his way to a window; pulling the curtains open to let faint starlight within. Yet he'd barely dumped his pack and removed his boots when the innkeeper returned with a light and a plate of cold mutton and water.

"That's all I could manage on such short notice, so I won't expect any complaints, will I?"

"A feast," he said, and started eating.

She clicked her tongue as she lit a flower-shaped lamp set in the wall and then left him to his meal.

Never ate most of the meat, setting it aside and taking a long drink before stretching out on the bed without bothering to remove any more of his clothes. The innkeeper didn't seem to want any attention from the monks, which made sense if she was involved with the rebels somehow, and which suggested she could be trusted not to turn him in overnight.

Hopefully.

There was no furniture to place before the door, so he had to make do with his pack. Yet a big part of him – too big, perhaps – didn't care. His weariness was swinging in; it'd knocked him into a welcome heaviness and the sensation of having eaten wasn't helping his alertness. He needed rest. Even what was left of the night and just half the morning would be enough...

It was noon when he woke, and it hadn't been enough. The racket from downstairs; the scrape of chairs, chatter, the sound of mugs thumping down onto wood, the music – all of it muted somewhat by the floor, but all of it enough to break his rest.

He rolled over, then jammed the pillow over his head to no avail.

"Fine."

Never sat up, reaching for his water. He drank, easing the dryness in his mouth and throat, but moving his head drove home his lack of rest. He was still groggy enough to consider lying back down with a silent promise to throttle the drummer below later on.

Instead, he dragged himself to the window. Across the way, almost close enough to reach, was the window of another building, curtains drawn. He looked down to the busy street, half-watching the men and women in their cinched robes. At least he hadn't been turned over to the monks. More than a few of the people below also wore coloured collars – a little reminiscent of the port dwellers in Hanik, only these were not jaunty scarves. The collars were more drab in colour.

But they were no slaves, not by the way they moved freely or the manner in which others regarded them. Yet even the pair of young men Never saw wearing collars, and who appeared to have some manner of servant following them, made way for a single monk in black robes. He wore a tyrant at his waist and a short bow across his back.

The warrior did not approach the inn and was quickly lost from sight.

Never returned to the bed and pulled on his boots. Time to find the innkeeper and, hopefully, the rebel leader Wanatek.

Downstairs, his entrance elicited an audible reduction in the talk and even the drummer missed a beat. A serving girl gaped at him a moment before offering to take his order, running her words together. By the glares he was getting from some of the patrons, he instead asked for the innkeeper.

"Mrs Ku is in the kitchen," she said after several attempts. Her raven hair was shaven high on the sides, leaving a generous streak tied back into a tail.

Never offered a smile; he'd obviously rattled the poor girl.

"I can wait outside if you like?"

The kitchen door swung open and Mrs Ku fixed him with her stern gaze. "Send him to the stables, Meia."

"Yes, madam."

Meia led Never to a narrow corridor beneath the staircase, then gestured to the stables that lay beyond a small yard of packed earth. He strolled across it; each stall had a horse munching on hay and a lad dashed between them.

The boy greeted Never cheerfully, though he did not start a conversation – but Mrs Ku appeared after only moments. "Thank you for last night," Never said.

"We'll see if it comes back to bite me, yet," she said, then raised a grey eyebrow. "Well?"

"I'm hoping you can help me find someone – I believe his name is Wanatek."

Mrs Ku folded her arms over her apron. "Do you?"

"Yes. If you could save me wandering the forest, I'd be grateful."

Mrs Ku gestured to the boy, who dropped his pail and ran back toward the main buildings. Never watched him, then looked back to the innkeeper. "Obedient lad you have there."

"Listen, stranger. You'd better have a good reason for asking after Wanatek; it'd be worth your life and my inn if the wrong ears hear you."

Good. Captain Milagra had been right. "Well, my reason's noble enough if that's what you need – I'm looking for a young woman of Marlosi heritage, she would have been kept in the temples, *somewhere* in Kiymako. I can't find anyone to help me and I don't fancy my chances simply asking at the first temple I find."

"And you think Wanatek can help you?" She gave no indication as to what she thought of his story.

"I figure if anyone would know of such secrets, or be willing to help me avoid notice from the Isansho and the monks, it'd be a wily rebel."

She muttered to herself. "Stay here; someone will see you."

"Someone?"

"Yes." And then she turned back across the yard.

Never started to pace. Stretching his wings would have been nice too but that might have been a bit much. He ate from his trail rations and drank from a water barrel in the corner of the yard while he waited, eventually sitting against the wall of the inn.

He tapped a foot. He *had* to be on the right path.

Hope stirred anew and he almost frowned. Too many times before, hope had been an enemy – a bitter spectre, robed in the possibility of success... Old lessons warned him against it but Father hadn't painted the rune on the temple door for nothing. She had to be here, had to be alive.

"Foreigner."

The voice came from above.

Never stood, glancing up to the roof tiles. A figure crouched before the edge, a mere shadow as he was positioned in such a way to keep the sun behind him.

"My name is Never. Who are you?"

"Muka. Tell me why you wish to speak to my master."

"I need his help finding someone that I believe has been imprisoned in the temples. She would have Marlosi heritage. In that, I believe we share a common adversary."

"Is that so, Never from Marlosi?"

"Will you deliver my request to meet?"

The figure rose, still mostly a silhouette. Was there a hint of a silvery beard as he turned his head, or was it just the light? "I do not believe so, stranger. But I will leave you with a word of advice – leave Kiymako while you still can."

And then he was gone.

Never swore. He leapt for the water barrel and used it to vault himself up to the edge of the wall which encircled the stable. From there, he climbed onto the inn's rooftop and shaded his eyes.

The man – and Never's best lead so far – was already several rooves away. "Damn him."

Never took a running leap, thudding onto the next building, keeping his footing on the tiles. The rooves weren't as easy to traverse compared to those of the Imperial City or other towns in Marlosi, but Never was doing well enough.

He threw himself across another gap, but he wasn't gaining.

Muka was simply too fast.

The rebel had already slipped out of sight, disappearing beyond a large, three storey building.

A hoarse shout echoed.

Men in black robes were circling below, a dozen in all. Most held drawn bows, others stood with hands on the hilts of their *sisan*. One of the monks appeared to have some sort of seniority judging from the elaborate flame symbol over his chest.

"Halt!" he cried. "Come down peacefully now."

Never glanced around; the building was well and truly surrounded.

"Listen well, foreigner. If you don't do as instructed you're coming down full of arrows. What will it be?" He waved his arms as he spoke, pointing to Never and then the ground.

With a sigh, Never raised his hands.

Chapter 10

Isansho Shika regarded him with some curiosity from where she stood before her easel, paintbrush in hand. She glanced at him often as she worked, her square jaw set in concentration and her dark hair shaved high at the sides, like every other woman Never had seen so far in the city.

However, unlike the other women, the overlord's hair bore traces of green paint, as did her hands and forearms where they slipped free of her dark robe. She still wore twin blades at her hip, one shorter than the other, but nothing ornamental to suggest she was a ruler of Najin.

Of course, sitting on a stool, hands bound, while someone painted his portrait was unusual enough to suggest that he was currently at the mercy of *someone* powerful. It was oddly intimate – unnerving even, since no-one had ever had need to paint him before.

"You have an arresting face, Never," she said.

"Thank you, Isansho." He glanced to the two bodyguards who stood just beyond the lantern-light. Were they really as fast as Hanael said? One stood near enough to a lacquered table that he could reach for a cup of something every now and then, the other was closer to the open shutters on the window, these too made of treated bamboo.

Escape certainly didn't seem likely – and maybe it wouldn't need to be. If he could talk his way into some sort of advantage...

"Lei-Dahn disapproves of my little habit, you see," Shika continued, frowning at her work. "He would prefer you were interrogated immediately."

"I imagine you're learning quite a lot in your own way, My Lady," he said. "He is the Gathering Monk?"

"He is." She changed brushes, taking blue paint now. "And I don't believe I have learnt enough, just yet. You are obviously Marlosi by your accent and colouring of course but there is something else to your features that I cannot place. And you are searching for someone; you worry. I see that in your eyes."

Never raised an eyebrow. He was yet to explain his purpose in Kiymako to his captors – yet, when had he grown so easy to read? "That is true, Isansho."

"And what makes you believe you will find them in Najin?"

"Hope."

She murmured as she made another few strokes before placing the brush down a moment. She stood back from the work. "Never, it is only a fool who plots a course on hope alone."

"I'm rather lucky, I have to admit."

Shika chuckled. "That I can see."

"I appear luckier when I'm not tied to a chair."

"Tell me, who were you chasing across the rooftops?"

"Someone who was supposed to help me find a pass," he

said smoothly.

"Oh? You're heading inland then?"

"Not any more it seems."

Shika shook her head. "An answer that is not an answer is hardly adequate, Never."

"Then may I ask you a question instead?"

"Please." She appeared amused.

"Don't you think I make a terrible spy? Or assassin, or whatever it is you assume I am?"

"Perhaps, but you've got yourself within these walls easily enough."

Now Never grinned. If only she knew how easy such a feat *could* have been. "Something that would be more impressive if I hadn't been given an armed escort."

She approached him now, but made no threatening move. Up close, he could see she was a little older than he'd first assumed, though not by much. "I must at least credit Wanatek for thinking outside his regular cast for infiltrators. But I do wonder what he offered you, since you have so little with you. Weren't you smart enough to demand payment up front? Or have you stashed it away somewhere."

Never hesitated. Was there an opportunity here? Perhaps, if he could play it right... "Are you offering more, Isansho?"

She frowned. "More?"

"Well, I find myself suddenly open to new arrangements – and surely I'm most ideally suited to gathering whatever information about Wanatek it is you're looking for."

"The man who takes silver from two employers leaves behind two knives."

"What if I didn't want silver?"

"Oh?"

"What if I wanted information?"

"Ah, we're travelling in circles now."

"About a girl – or a young woman – of Marlosi heritage, who was raised or possibly held prisoner in a temple."

Lady Shika studied him for a long moment. "That is a very dangerous question to ask."

"Do you not ask something very dangerous of me in return?"

"I do." She folded her arms, then turned and strode to her men, speaking softly. Then, they started forward, faces impassive when they reached the light. One gestured for Never to stand, and then he was being half-carried, half-led from the room and into a dim corridor.

Shika trailed without a word.

Never kept his hands together, his nails poised to gouge his palm, just in case. Crimson-fire would dissolve his bindings, and give him a chance of escape, but he still hadn't had a chance to take the measure of his captors.

And more, there was a chance Shika would help him.

When they came to steps leading up to a curtain, the bodyguards stopped. One pulled him aside, allowing Shika to draw it open. She turned to look down on Never.

"Few see this room and live, Never. Touch nothing, understood?"

"Understood."

She motioned to her men and Never was released. He started up the steps, following Shika into the room, her bodyguards close behind.

The overseer was lighting evenly-spaced lamps, seeing as there were no windows. It was a large, square room with little furniture, only two long cabinets around waist high, mostly made of glass.

But it was the walls that caught his eye.

Dozens of paintings lined the room, all uniform in shape but covering the entire spectrum of colour. And they started with a deep purple, near black, and lightened and changed as they progressed around the room.

The first was difficult to discern, but the second was rendered more clearly – a corpse. The purples bled into one another but the sightless gaze and sunken cheeks were clear. Its torso appeared to bear hints of red too.

"My memory, as best I can manage, of my first encounter with death."

"A chilling image."

She appeared pleased. "There is one in particular I wish you to see. Come." Shika led him around the room, slow enough that he had a chance to see many more faces. Some were still alive while painted – expressions of anger, defiance or defeat clear. Where Shika had included a setting, it was the room Never had himself sat within moments before.

One man, who'd been shown mostly in yellows, was repeated in three paintings. Each time, he slumped further on the stool... as if she had painted his actual death.

Never stopped.

"Traitors, murderers and criminals mostly," she said when she turned back to him.

"And the others?"

"Sometimes merely a face I wished to capture," she said with a shrug. "Quickly now."

Never joined her at the first cabinet; it was filled with a wide assortment of items, all arranged on black cloth. A piece of pottery, a single playing card, a river stone, a silver dagger and various other items – one of which was a ring set with a small ruby stone.

Hanael's ring?

"Here."

Never looked up.

The young girl stood in pinks and reds, her dark eyes and black, waist-length hair vivid in the image. Unlike the other pictures, which had been created using heavier paints and strokes, this seemed to be done with a softer approach.

Her expression was one of deep weariness, though she still might have been called 'cute' rather than pretty – doubtless because she was young.

He could not look away.

Could the girl... he raised a hand but did not reach out. Something about her expression... the closer he looked the more it seemed possible. Her features suggested mixed heritage, her skin tone a little darker than common in Kiymako and her mouth, something about it was familiar.

Like Father.

Never spun. "Who is she? Tell me. Is she alive?"

Shika lifted a finger. "I do not care for your tone, Never. But yes, she lives."

"Forgive me, Isansho, but I must know more."

"And so you shall – when I get what you have promised and no sooner."

Chapter 11

Never knelt within a bamboo grove set off the path, the deep-green tunic he'd been given spread between two trees. Cool, evening air prickled his bare skin as he lifted his blade and made two incisions in the cloth for his wings.

He stopped before replacing the garment. The five-pointed leaf of the Amouni symbol glowed beneath the skin on his chest again. How long since it had last done so? It flared twice then disappeared, leaving him no closer to understanding it. Was it supposed to be a warning? He frowned as he pulled his tunic over his head then replaced his pack and set off once more.

It had taken the rest of the day to lose whoever Shika had sent to tail him, as best he could tell, and now he was finally rejoining more well-travelled roads. He'd already been stopped twice by warrior monks, but the pass – coupled with the Isansho's talon-seal – was enough to let him continue unhampered.

Sometime tomorrow he'd reach a section of the Najin Forest where recent skirmishes with the rebels had taken place. Finding them would be its own problem, but that was just one part of the price of his bluff. Lady Shika's demands were another – her words had burned with a need, a hatred it seemed she'd been unable to control; she wanted Wanatek destroyed. *I suspect a coup. Find the truth of the matter and deliver to me every detail. Every detail – for I mean to crush them now, finally. Every man and woman, every shuddering final breath will be mine to relish.*

If he could manage that, she'd tell him what else she knew about the girl who *had* to be his sister.

There was always a chance he was wrong. Her supposed Marlosi features didn't automatically make her his sister. The girl could have been anyone. A figment of Shika's fertile – and morbid – imagination even.

But it didn't feel that way.

"Pacela be kind," he muttered as he moved deeper into the forest, his footfalls swallowed by the loam. Travelling east, the setting sun pushed him on, long shadows leading eventually to a moss-covered bridge. Never slowed as he approached; the wooden structure was wide enough for two abreast only and the further it extended, the sharper the earth below fell away.

It was deserted, the trees empty and the sloping ground appearing to conceal no surprises... he took his first few steps, one hand on the rope rail. At first, the bridge spanned a small drop, but as he walked its length, the ground fell further and further away. Streams appeared below, whispering as he walked. Ahead, the bridge maintained an even level, but the support beams disappeared and instead, it was now affixed to the stronger, bigger bamboo trees.

The rushing of streams grew louder as he neared the

centre.

At its opposite end, some distance away yet, the ground sloped up once more, rather steeply. It seemed the entire bridge had been made to not only bypass the fractured streams but to save travellers a sharp climb. Very considerate.

Below, orange glimmered in the water; the light almost playful.

A figure stood in the middle of the bridge when Never looked back up.

He stopped.

The man stood, arms folded against his dark tunic, a tyrant strapped across his back, the grip big enough for two hands. He offered no words when Never resumed his trek across the bridge. The stranger wore no hood, revealing silvery hair and beard and a dispassionate expression that did not change when Never stopped once again, now no more than ten feet away.

"Do I have to guess a secret word before you let me pass?"

"Turn back, Never from Marlosi." His voice was deep, familiar. The man from the inn... Muka? The fellow hadn't made any threatening move yet, aside from his stance and decidedly unwelcoming tone.

"I have come too far."

"But you will go no further if you pursue such folly. Wanatek will not see you, especially now that you have been released from the snake-pit."

"I owe her nothing."

Muka stepped back, drawing the *sisan*. "Leave this place."

Never drew his daggers. He was overmatched when it came to steel alone... but there was a chance that this man and his master could help. Killing Muka now, with crimson-fire or by draining the man of his blood, would hardly help his cause. "I do not wish to harm you."

Now Muka smiled faintly. "I cannot say the same."

He swung his blade. It whistled in the air. Never sprang back, flinging a knife at the man's leg. Muka deflected it with his sword then frowned at Never. "Do me the courtesy of fighting to kill."

Never drew another knife, he was down to six, and charged. Muka leapt to meet him, swinging his blade in a mighty overhand blow. The sword flashed with the setting sun. Never twisted and the blade grazed his forearm on its way down. Muka reversed the weapon before it hit the bridge, jabbing backwards but Never was already dropping into a crouch, jerking his head to the side.

Muka spun, slashing downward.

Never crossed his blades. He caught the tyrant with a grunt and shoved back, using his legs to drive himself up, and Muka away. The man stumbled as their weapons came free then Never was feinting a throw with his left dagger. Instead, he flicked the knife with his right hand but again, Muka deflected it before attacking once more.

On the narrow bridge, Never was forced to give ground. He fell back, coming up against the rail.

Muka lunged.

Never leapt over the rope, gripping bamboo and swinging out over the open air, whipping around to thump onto the bridge behind the swordsman. The stunt had put him on the wrong side of the span but it gave him enough time to spring up into the branches of another, sturdier tree.

There, he let his wings burst free before kicking off, ascending quickly. Below, Muka stared up in shock, the blade hanging loosely in his hands.

"Try not to take this personally," Never shouted as he broke free of the canopy in a shower of leaves.

Below, Muka charged along the bridge but it was clear he couldn't keep up forever. Never beat his wings harder, gaining enough height that he could study wide swathes of forest below at a glance.

Just how far had Muka travelled to intercept? He would have wanted to head off any chance of Never stumbling across any rebel camp but also likely not have travelled so far that he couldn't return before full dark.

Even now the light was failing, leaving less and less for Never to focus on in the trees below. And even if he found any such camp, it was clear he'd have a hard time convincing them to help. Perhaps a grand gesture was in order, more so even than the little shock he gave Muka.

Below, a hint of light caught his eye. No smoke, the wood burned clean, but it was a camp fire of some sort, deep in a depression within the forest. No doubt well-concealed from anyone on foot but Wanatek had no way to know he'd be contending with eyes in the sky.

Never angled toward the camp, drawing one of his remaining knives as he did.

He sliced a thin cut along the back of each hand, letting the blood run and extend into twin globes of burning crimson. Then he swooped low over the camp and lashed out with a narrow stream of fire.

It tore through the canopy and into the trunk of a bamboo tree, which toppled to the earth. Shouts of alarm rose from tents in the large clearing and the very trees themselves. Never hesitated, hovering as he found another target – which was hopefully empty, and sliced again.

This tree fell across the camp fire but a figure in black darted from cover to remove it before smoke could rise.

Never swooped low and thundered to the earth. He hit hard, dust rising, jolts running up his legs but he ignored the pain, instead shouting for Wanatek.

Men and women rose from where they'd fallen back, their eyes wide. He flared the crimson-fire, pointing a burning hand at the nearest fellow, an archer whose arrow had fallen to the dirt. "Bring me Wanatek. Now." He kept his voice low.

The man ran for the edge of the clearing.

Other rebels stood motionless, though many – too many – still held their weapons. Some bore tyrants or twin blades, others carried bows. None appeared so different from their counterparts in Najin, if he overlooked an additional wear to their tunics and robes. A few had remained in the trees and were watching him from their vantage points. None had drawn a bead on him, but it wouldn't take long – shock would wear off.

He could replace it with fear if he engulfed one of them in flame... but that would create as many problems as it solved.

"I am Wanatek," a voice announced.

A slender man with a fox-like face approached from the trees, his expression one of concern. He hid his surprise better than his fellows when he saw Never, taking in the wings and the fire, only a slight widening of his eyes. His tunic was cinched with a silver belt, which bore only a dagger. The rebel leader stood some distance away. "Is Muka alive?"

"Yes."

Wanatek knelt. "Thank you for granting him your mercy, Son of the Phoenix."

Chapter 12

Wanatek handed a steaming cup across the small table. "It is peppermint tea, Chosen of the Phoenix."

Never accepted the cup with a sigh. "Please, Wanatek. You know I am no such thing – why would your land's most magical creature choose a Marlosi man? We both know it makes no sense."

He smiled, adding warmth to his sharp features. "I am aware of that – but you are hardly Marlosi alone. Ancient blood runs in your veins, does it not?"

Never paused. "You know of the Amouni?"

One of the attendants, a short woman by the name of Etsu shifted her feet where she stood in the tent's entry, her back to the soft lamp that illuminated the sparse pavilion. She, like the rest of the camp, had rarely spoken to Never since Wanatek's display, instead treating Never with a timid reverence.

Useful, but ultimately unwelcome – it was too much a glimpse of the world Snow had wanted.

"Of course. Few believe, treating them as myth only – and

foreign myth at that," he said, taking a drink from his own cup. "But the temple keeps the Amouni and their role in creating the first Great Phoenix secret."

"Creating...?" Never shook his head. It wasn't so hard to believe, truly, but he couldn't let such a revelation move his focus. "Even if that is so, I am not here to lead, guide or punish anyone. I am seeking help."

He nodded. "You are guided, no change before struggle."

"I cannot help with your rebellion, Wanatek."

"Najin's rebellion," he said, his expression darkening. "I understand you have met Lady Shika? Did you see her... collection?"

"I did."

"She is not fit. That is something all must come to believe, as you and I know. I must break the spell she has cast."

"She expects a coup."

"Perhaps in time, but my goals are both more immediate and more long-term and not something I will burden you with, Chosen One. How can I help you?"

Never set his cup down. "I have heard you once served the temples."

"Yes." His expression revealed no emotion.

"I am searching for someone and I believe she has been imprisoned or maybe only raised by the temple. She would appear at least somewhat as Marlosi."

"Ah." Now the man's tone was one of regret. "I know of whom you speak; she was being held in the Divine Temple of Mondami when I served, but that was three years gone."

Never leant forward. Finally! The girl's existence was confirmed but he still needed proof of their kinship. "But she was alive then?"

He nodded.

"And was she well? Do you know if they mistreat her? Or why they hold her?"

"I never saw her myself, but I doubt she would have been mistreated as a matter of course – the temple protects her; Ayuni is their most treasured possession."

"What?" A flash of anger lent heat to his words and it took a moment for him to register something – he knew the girls name now. Ayuni – a beautiful name.

Never apologised.

"No need to seek forgiveness," he said. "I hardly know her story, but she is transferred from city to city on a hidden schedule, where she performs some duty. Ayuni was only in Najin Temple for four days at a time – always in spring."

Never stood. This was more than he'd learnt since arriving in Kiymako. "Do you know where she would travel next?"

He nodded. "If her routine still holds, she would have gone to Takbisu City next, I believe."

Never closed his eyes a moment... the map, it had put Takbisu nearby – northwest. On the shores of the giant lake. The second largest city in Kiymako, a large central temple one of dozens. "Thank you for the hospitality."

Wanatek stood. "You cannot go now, Chosen One – the roads at night are unkind."

He grinned. "But the skies tend to be open."

"But you need a guide. And rest. Leave tomorrow, I will send someone familiar with Takbisu to assist you. It will be my honour to help."

Never glanced into the darkness beyond the tent flap and the guard. Was it such a poor idea? A good night's sleep would be welcome, and the rebels were both well-hidden and seemed diligent when it came to remaining that way. They had to be.

"Thank you."

"Etsu will arrange a tent," he said, glancing to the guard, who slipped away without a word. The rebel leader hesitated. "Might I ask a boon of you, Chosen One?"

"My name is 'Never', remember?"

"Of course."

Never hung his head with a sigh; the man had no intention of using it. "Go ahead."

"When you meet the Great Phoenix, if it isn't presumptuous of me, I would like you to ask for her Blessing. My cause is just but it would set my mind at ease."

"When?"

"Yes." He offered a calm smile.

Never shrugged. "Very well, I won't argue with your conviction. *If* I meet the Great Phoenix I'll ask for a blessing for you."

He went to his knees once more before rising. "Thank you, Chosen One."

Etsu returned, speaking softly. Never followed her out and across the camp, heading to a small tent. She gave a nervous smile and gestured within. "I hope this is comfortable."

"It's fine, please don't worry about me," Never said.

She nodded and hurried back toward Wanatek's pavilion. Never slipped inside and lay on the borrowed blankets. How soon was morning? If his Amouni blood offered the ability to see through darkness along with its other dubious gifts, he'd already be on the road. From memory, Takbisu was over a week *around* the forest. A boat across the lake would be quicker. Is that what Wanatek had in mind?

It was more than hope – it was a strange conviction that told him Ayuni was the sister he sought. From where such certainty came he did not wish to question but it was almost as if his very blood was trying to tell him he had almost found her.

He had to trust it until he was proven right or wrong.

But would Ayuni still be in the city? The season was right... but more pressing... was she well? And just what were the monks using her for? If it was her blood and the exchange of knowledge, like the Amouni of old, that would have been a chore but potentially not so damaging as any number of other unsavoury things they might be up to.

Had she tried to leave already?

Who watched her and under what conditions did she travel? It seemed the easiest time to free her, compared to breaking into the temple. Not that he wouldn't try. If she was even there. If she was still being 'used' and if the girl Wanatek had seen was truly Ayuni. Never muttered a curse. If, if, if.

"Sweet Gods Above, how am I meant to sleep?"

***

Never paced within the tree line.

Only Wanatek and Muka had made the journey north to the edge of Takbisu Lake; it glittered between the trunks like a pristine field empty of tree or shrub, just an expanse of deep blue. Stands of young bamboo were visible near the shore, but it was mostly clear – save for the small figure of Muka as he rowed toward them.

The city of Takbisu was still well and truly beyond sight

but knowing it was close was enough to stop Never adding a stream of curses beneath his breath as he paced.

"See? Muka nears, trust him," Wanatek said.

"Let's hope that's a sailboat – I'd hate to have to row the whole way." Never stopped to lean against a tree, folding his arms and tapping a finger against his bicep.

"You worry about the temple."

"A little. But your help has been invaluable." The rebel leader, along with others no doubt, had sacrificed sleep to create disguises, both for the road and for the possibility of infiltrating the temples. He could not carry the clothing in his own pack – that was still in the Green Leaf Inn but Wanatek was going to retrieve it for him, thankfully. But all disguises aside, his accent would likely give him away so Muka would have had to do most of the talking.

Still, it was more than Never had expected.

"It is our pleasure, Chosen One."

Never didn't bother correcting him – he'd already tried twelve times on their trek north – instead, he asked a question that had been weighing upon him. "In your time with the temple, did you get to know many of your fellow monks? I know there are so many, but this man would have held some manner of rank."

"I believe so, why?"

"Because when I first arrived in Kiymako, I visited a fishing village east of Najin and met an old monk. He led me astray; it nearly cost me my life."

Wanatek straightened. "His name?"

"Hiruso."

The rebel leader drew in a breath. "Be wary. Brother Hiruso is a dangerous man – perhaps more than a man, at that."

"How so?"

"Hiruso is the Head of the Temples, the Hand of the Phoenix. He can commit acts that may trouble even someone Chosen as you. He leads a powerful faction that influences many, even the Divine Throne. It is my belief that he would not wish to see Amouni blood on Kiymako soil unless it had been spilled."

Never clenched a fist. Then the bastard *had* sent him to the Sundered Road to be killed. "I have to wonder what he was doing so far from the capital?"

"I cannot say. His motives are obtuse at the best of times." A slight frown marred his brow. "Perhaps he has come so far south to watch me, perhaps to continue to oversee the closing of the harbour. Or perhaps he was here for you."

"Me?"

He shook his head. "I cannot say. He is enigmatic, and I fear the temple does not truly understand him in any event."

"Wonderful; a new enemy." If the man was so unpredictable, so powerful, who did he answer to? Could he have known Never would land near that village, and been prepared? One thing Never was now certain of, Hiruso knew exactly where to find Ayuni.

"Not if you avoid him as I suggest."

Muka had grown large enough to see that his boat was a small sloop with a single sail. A rising wind was slowing him, but he would arrive soon enough. "Ready?" Wanatek asked.

"Very much so."

He followed the rebel leader from the trees and onto the shore, his feet sinking in the sandy earth a little. No pier had been erected here, so far from any villages, so Never and Wanatek waded into the cool water to help haul the sloop up onto the beach.

Never loaded his new pack and provisions into the boat while Muka and Wanatek spoke quietly. Wanatek placed a hand on the bigger man's shoulder. "The Goddess watches over me, worry not."

Muka's expression was not one of confidence but he returned to the boat and helped push it into the shallows before leaping inside. Never joined him, leaving only Wanatek standing waist-deep in the water.

"Seek Niswan, she will help you," he called.

Never waved his thanks.

Muka was making small adjustments to the sail, which was collecting the rising breeze. So far, he had not spoken. In fact, the last words he'd directed to Never had been during their scuffle on the bridge.

"Shall I row first?" Never asked.

The man nodded.

Never took each oar and arranged them across his knees. He paused before fitting them to the locks. "From what I could tell, Shika doesn't know enough to trouble Wanatek."

He glanced at Never a moment. "Thank you. My concern is actually more for Lord Wanatek – his boldness can be both a blessing and a curse."

"He's not planning a coup, however, is he?"

"Not as Shika would expect," Muka replied, but did not offer any more.

Never didn't press. "I appreciate you helping me. It wasn't my intent to take you from your purpose in Najin."

"That I know. I will help you because Wanatek wills it."

He hesitated. "And because I cannot deny, after seeing your wings, that you are more than you appear."

"I only want to find my sister."

"If she is the young lady Wanatek believes her to be, then I will do what I can to help you."

"Thank you, Muka." Never dipped the oars into the water. His first few strokes were a struggle as he didn't find rhythm quickly, but the breeze assisted and they began to make good speed.

"How long to Takbisu?" he asked during a moment of rest. The lake stretched on, only one shore visible to his left. Takbisu was northeast but the exact distances were unclear, since the map he'd seen had been written in Kiymako.

"We should reach the shore tonight if we row through."

"Can we dock safely?"

"I believe so. In any event, it will be a fine test of your disguise."

"Comforting," Never said with a grin. "What of Niswan? How do we find her?"

"Her store is across from the sun dial in the Fabric Quarter."

"She's a tailor?"

"The best in the city."

Never resumed rowing. "Wanatek didn't explain how she could help."

"She will know if your sister has been in the city recently. It is her responsibility to create the garments for temple."

"Garments?"

"I do not understand myself, but Wanatek tells me that is one of her duties. She must make special clothing for the temple every spring."

Oddly ominous – yet he could not establish why. "Then I would very much like to speak with her."

Chapter 13

Moonlight rippled across the lake's surface, casting everything a cool blue. The other boats and ships, most with sails furled and few with glowing lights, rocked gently where they were docked. Takbisu Harbour was a mixture of old stone and freshly cut wood, rope leading from the ships to mooring posts, looking not unlike dark spider webs sagging beneath the weight of the night.

"Remember to let me speak," Muka whispered.

Never nodded as he rubbed at his aching back, though the man may not have seen it as they climbed from the sloop and started along the pier. The city was quiet this late, even at the waterfront. What it lacked in music or voices, it made up for with the scent of old fish guts and seaweed. No wall greeted them as they neared the end of the boardwalk, but a lamp glowed over a doorway to a guard post, revealing a guard.

The man wore a tyrant and moved to block their path as they approached.

"Please state your purpose."

"Returning to temple," Muka said.

The man gave a nod, having already seemed to have noted their temple robes, and waved both within. Never strode beside Muka up the paved street, passing through shadows between large buildings – warehouses mostly, it seemed.

"Was it really that easy?" Never asked.

"He had little reason to doubt us," Muka said. "Monks are rarely challenged, since they are the final authority on many matters. However, he will inform the nearest temple of our entry as a matter of routine."

"Will that cause us any problems?"

"Had I given a specific temple, possibly."

He nodded slowly. "So the monks report in to their own temples like a military organisation?"

"Somewhat. For anyone attempting to find us after the guard's report, they must search *all* temples – and there are two dozen in Takbisu – and then the streets."

"Seamless."

"For now. If we are challenged directly, things may turn ugly." He stopped before a narrow opening between two buildings – both inns, it seemed. "This will save some time."

He led Never through the darkness, where they encountered none of the normal refuse Never might have expected from Marlosi or Hanik back streets. Once a cat gave a hiss as they disturbed it with their passage but nothing else of note occurred until they exited into a tiny square that led to rear doors of several buildings.

A well waited in the quiet, and nearby a dark figure stood with a pipe. Smoke lifted gently, seeming to gather the moonlight.

Muka did not greet him and nor did the fellow offer any

words of his own.

They travelled through several backstreets in a similar way, which prevented Never from getting a real sense of Takbisu. Even when they stopped at the rear of what Muka assured him was Niswan's store, Never couldn't find any difference between it and the other buildings – especially as the moon was now hidden from view.

"I fear I must wake her and she will not be pleased," Muka said, though the tone of his voice suggested that he would not be too troubled by it. Perhaps they were old friends.

He rapped on a heavy door until a light in a room on the second floor appeared.

Soon after, the thud of feet on stairs followed and then the click of a key in a lock. The door jerked open, lamplight revealing a woman wearing a deep frown. Her hair had been pulled up into a topknot, revealing the shaven part of her head. She held a serious-looking baton in one hand.

"If you don't stop that—"

"Good evening, Niswan," Muka said.

Her expression became almost comical in its surprise. "Muka?" She leapt into his arms and Never noted that her feet were bare. Then she stepped back and slapped the warrior, not too hard, but enough to express her displeasure it seemed. "You couldn't wait a few more hours for dawn?"

"It's urgent."

She turned her gaze to Never, eyes widening. "Who's this?"

"My name is Never, forgive me for interrupting your rest," he said. He lowered his voice. "Wanatek believes you can help me."

Niswan gave him a look, then waved her weapon with a

sigh. "Then you'd better come in, Never."

She led them to a darkened kitchen, stirring the flames within an oven and lighting a lamp. Herbs hung from the roof beams and pots too, but it was the table that caught his eye. It was covered in pieces of cloth and rolls of thread, a swatch of needles gleaming in the light.

"There's only two chairs, so one of you is standing," she said as she took the nearest, setting her weapon down to rub at her eyes. "And this better be good, Muka. I was having a spectacular dream; a rich client had left their purse behind and it was full of gold crescents. Full. I was on my way to the upper markets to buy –"

"It is." Muka gestured for Never to sit as he answered.

"Wanatek tells me you are the best seamstress in Takbisu and that you create special clothing for someone who visits the temple," Never began.

She nodded. "He's underestimating me, but the other thing is true. What does it matter?"

"Are you making anything now?"

"I am – the usual robe. It's for a young woman, it's mostly pinks and white. Sometimes I add a rose trim." She paused. "I don't think it'd fit you, stranger."

More luck! Perhaps Pacela was guiding his steps after all – about time. He grinned. "Nor I. When will you deliver it?"

She leaned back in the chair, looking from Never to Muka. "What is this about? I'm not interested in anything that will lose me that contract. The temple pays well. And swiftly."

"That won't happen," Never said. "Information is help enough – it's up to me to free her."

Niswan chuckled. "You've got guts – no brains, but guts

at least."

"He could probably do it, Ni," Muka said.

"You think so? Then you're as stupid as him," she said. "Whoever I make that robe for is surrounded by half a dozen bodyguards at all times and no foreigner is getting into any temple. And the monks send her between temples in a steel box, like a cage but with only a tiny window. I've seen it once. You think you can deal with all of that?"

"I have to," Never said. "She's my sister."

Niswan narrowed her eyes. "Now you're joking, right?"

"You tell me. Have you seen her?"

"Once. Last year, during delivery." Niswan scratched at her hair. "She was weary-looking; I've never seen anyone look that exhausted. Maybe her skin was a little darker than ours but I assumed she was from north but now that you ask me... she *might* have had something of a Marlosi look about her."

"Her name is Ayuni and she's my half-sister. She's a prisoner," Never said. He kept his voice firm. "I am going to free her."

Niswan spread her hands. "Honestly, I hope you do... but I can't see how."

"Just tell me when she's leaving; I can manage the rest."

"Generally, the morning I deliver – which is three days from now, actually." She yawned.

"Perfect. One more question, what is strange about the robe you make?"

"Oh. That, the temple always wants it to be waterproof, which *is* odd because the process ruins the silk in the end."

Never clenched a fist, keeping it beneath the table.

Waterproofing meant blood. For anyone else it would

have been a protection against the rain but Ayuni was Amouni. They were using her blood somehow. That was why when Niswan had seen her in the morning, she was exhausted.

Bastards.

The monks were bleeding her... but for what?

Chapter 14

Never spent most of the next day hidden in Niswan's kitchen, letting Muka collect any supplies they needed and undertake preliminary scouting, both around the 'Great' Temple and the roads in and out of the city. Niswan couldn't recall which direction the steel cage had been heading in when she'd seen it, but she thought north.

Which probably meant it had been on its way to Mondami. According to his host, good roads led to the capital through open fields for the most part. Few opportunities for ambush.

Footsteps in the hallway approached. Never looked up from his bowl of diced fish.

Niswan appeared, her hair neater today, but her expression troubled. "You have to leave."

He stood. "Is someone here?"

"Not any more but I just had a visitor – the temple wants the dress today. I think they're leaving earlier than usual; I've sent for Muka."

"Has he returned to the city already?"

"I hope so. My messenger is starting with the Divine Temple."

"And you haven't delivered the dress yet?"

"Not yet. Why?"

"Maybe Muka and I should escort you."

She folded her arms. "I'm not going to agree to that; it puts me in too much danger. Stick with your other plan."

"Plans are made to be altered," he said as he collected his borrowed pack from a corner and started rifling through it. At the bottom, he found the map Wanatek had drawn for him. "How many exits from the Divine Temple?"

"Three."

"One to the north?"

"Yes. Why, Never?"

He tapped a finger on the image that represented Mondami. "They're taking Ayuni back to the capital."

"You can't know that – they might head east to Yalinamo, she is apparently sent between all temples."

"No, I need to be at the northern exit to the temple or even the city, that's where they're taking her."

"You're gambling."

He shook his head. "Brother Hiruso knows I'm here, he's rushing to move her."

Niswan raised an eyebrow. "Brother Hiruso is looking for you?"

"Doubtless."

"Then you'll need more than Muka's sword."

"I have a few surprises for the old monk, don't worry about that," Never said.

The echo of knocking came from the rear door. Never glanced to Niswan as he drew his knives, leading her down the passage where he stopped with a hand on the door.

A voice called from outside. "It's Muka."

Never let him in. "They're going to move her today."

He nodded. "We still have time, at least until Ni makes her delivery."

Niswan took them both back to the kitchen and paused at the doorway leading to the shopfront. "If Brother Hiruso is involved you can't rush anything. I have to finish the dress. Don't leave before I get a chance to see you again."

And then she was gone.

Muka moved to the basin and splashed water across his face. "I was only able to scout the east and north roads but there are little options for ambush in the rice fields. If they take her south, we could wait for them in the forest."

"I believe Brother Hiruso knows I'm seeking her. He'd take her back to the capital; we need to cover the northern highway."

"It's likely if you're right, but we are only two."

"Do you really think you're only worth one man, Muka?"

A faint smile. "And you?"

"Enough."

"Six bodyguards and the driver, along with the steel cage. It is a formidable task."

"I can cut through the steel easily enough – I assume Wanatek mentioned what I can do with fire?"

He nodded.

"Good. There's more. I don't like our chances if we simply follow all the way to Mondami waiting for a better place to ambush them. Especially if Hiruso has sent more men to escort her."

"True. But consider Hiruso – if he seeks you, what better way to draw you from hiding?"

Never began to pace. A troubling and very realistic

possibility – and one he should have considered. He'd been rushing, his fear leading him along. If Ayuni slipped away now and was then hidden deep in one of the temples... "We have to be ready for that possibility."

"How?"

Never stopped. "Is there anywhere in the city where we can watch the Divine Temple, and see more than one entrance?"

"The Watchtower of the Heavens," Muka said. "It is perfect."

"Can we use it?"

"We will find out."

Before they left, he and Muka changed back into regular travelling clothes so as not to draw attention and then Muka called for Niswan. Never lurked back in the hall, in case she had a customer. Best that he wasn't seen by too many people, and not just for her sake. She met them at the doorway, a needle between her teeth. "Here." She handed Muka a *sisan* sheathed in an ornate scabbard, the black surface covered in spidery golden images or words – Never couldn't be sure.

Muka pushed it back into her hands, gently. "I cannot accept this. It was your father's."

"He's not using it, is he?"

"That's not the point. It would not be right."

She shook her head. "You were his last student; no-one else is worthy. Go, take it and for the sake of every God in the Forest, be careful." To Never, she said, "If you let something happen to him I'll come after you, got it?"

"Got it."

Muka accepted the blade, exchanging it for his own, then started down the hall without a word. Never followed him from Niswan's home and into the backstreets, the shadows from the late afternoon sun deep.

But the daylight gave him his first real look at Takbisu as they moved through the streets, Never's hood raised, and hands in his pockets. The buildings were cut from a paler stone here, but many rooves were still of bamboo. Little seemed truly different save for symbols painted onto the doors, usually in white or sky-blue paint.

The image of his father painting on a temple flashed in his mind.

Had this been the city where he'd left her all those years ago?

He did not ask Muka about them, since he did not want to draw attention with his accent. And more, the man seemed possessed of a new dark mood. Was it the sword or the warning? There was obviously a history between Muka and Niswan's family.

Despite the desire to remain unobtrusive, Never found the people of Takbisu to be blessedly disinterested in he and Muka. Their voices provided a steady hum as they went about their business. More folk here wore the collars he'd seen in Najin, once again in a variety of colours. Another entry to his long list of questions.

Only once did Muka quicken their pace. "Ahead and to the left," he said as he turned into a side street. Never followed, catching a glimpse of a trio of warrior monks in their black, head bands keeping hair from their faces and tyrants at their belts. They seemed to be questioning a shopkeeper.

A narrow tower of stone and wood, not unlike a lighthouse, soon came into view above the tallest buildings. As they neared, Never saw that the wooden part was a platform on top, open to the air. For the study of the sky?

At the base, Muka rang a brass bell and stood back, waiting. A notice had been placed beside the door, illegible to Never. Much like many of the other buildings in the city, the wooden door had been painted with a symbol – a very simple image, a half circle connected to a straight line. Like the sun and the ocean. Rising or setting? He asked Muka about it after it became clear no-one was arriving to admit them in a hurry.

"Most houses have symbols to give thanks or beseech fortune from the Gods. It is mostly done here; Lake people are more superstitious than elsewhere."

"And on the temples?"

"No, the temple would consider it unbecoming."

Had father's painting of the Amouni rune for protection been as much an act of defiance as care, then? It suited the Amouni arrogance.

Muka reached for the bell once more, but before he could ring it, the door was opened. A balding man with wild eyebrows and an unshaven face held the door open with a welcoming smile. "Afternoon, seekers."

"Our apologies, but we are here to ask a favour, not to learn about the stars and the heavens."

"Oh? Well, please ask."

"I wish to show my travelling friend the city and thought that the viewing platform would be ideal."

The fellow blinked at Never. "Traveller, eh? Been up north for a while, I take it?"

"Yes," Never said. "I was surprised to hear the harbour was closed."

"Bah, foolishness from the Divine Throne. Those Vadiya blockheads have no reason to invade Kiymako, never did, and certainly not now." He shrugged. "Well, I'll let you head up. Hope you like stairs."

"Thank you," Muka said. "Your generosity will be noted at my temple."

He waved a hand. "Not to worry, big man."

Inside, the large circular room was divided into sections by shelving stuffed with books and scrolls. The old guy who'd admitted them headed for a long table, sitting across from another fellow who hadn't looked up from an abacus and ledger.

The stairs were well-worn in the centre as they circled the tower. Small windows let in warm, orange light in the absence of torches. At what he guessed was the halfway point, Never leant to look down on Takbisu.

His view was about level with a three-storey inn's roof. Atop, a small door led to a row of chairs. A symbol had been painted in white there too. Obviously, the Divine Temple was on the other side of the tower.

By the top, Never's calves were starting to strain, but he forgot once Muka took him to a sturdy wooden rail that lined the wide viewing platform.

The sinking sun sent its golden-orange rays racing across the mass of Lake Takbisu and into the city, splashing the walls and streets. Anyone not in direct sunlight was a dark shadow, the streets still busy enough.

But it was the Divine Temple that he studied.

Broad avenues led into the sprawling building, allowing a clear view of the north and east, and a somewhat obstructed view of the southern exit. The structure did not appear completely ornamental, but it was not quite militaristic either – no parapets, but small towers that lined the central, oval structure could certainly conceal archers.

A thin pattern of red stone contrasted with the pale limestone, appearing almost as a trim to the walls and towers. A similar-coloured glow echoed from the centre of the oval building, like a slumbering flame lurking beneath the large glass skylight. An entry point? He'd done it before.

The problem was, this time, he wouldn't know what to expect once he found himself inside.

"From here we can watch the north and east exits easily," Muka said. "South is a little harder, but we don't have a chance of seeing the west."

"This is enough," Never said. "And I can fly over to the west side if need be... though I'd make a lovely target against the setting sun."

"Then now we wait and watch."

Never sighed. "We should have carried up some chairs."

By twilight, little had changed below. Monks started trickling from all over the city, along with regular folk making their gratitude-reports, or perhaps half of them were spies. But no wagon with steel cage had left from any exit they could see, though Muka still worried about the western side of the Divine Temple.

"If I must, I can search that side of the city once it's a little darker," Never said. "I still feel that Hiruso will–"

"Look." Muka pointed down to the northern exit.

Never leant into the rail. A group of warriors were gathering before an arched opening, spreading out to allow a team of horses to pull a wagon through. As it moved, the bodyguards kept pace. A large, dark box sat on the wagon bed, appearing large enough to house a single person quite comfortably.

Was she truly inside or was it one of Hiruso's ploys?

"We need to let them leave the immediate area of the temple or reinforcements will overwhelm us," Muka said.

Never nodded. He tapped his foot as he watched the wagon make its steady way from the temple grounds, before turning north, just as he'd expected. By the time they climbed down, Ayuni would have made significant progress toward Takbisu's northern gate.

"Ready?" Muka asked.

He opened his mouth to reply but stopped.

Two robed figures, one taller than the other, were flitting from the southern exit.

Chapter 15

"Grab on," Never cried.

Muka blinked.

"Take my hands, we're going after them – the cage is a fake." Never let his wings burst free, a pair of black feathers drifting to the wood.

"I see them but..." Muka's eyes were wide. "I'm too heavy, surely?"

Admittedly, the man was bigger than Elina and in carrying her Never had possessed a higher starting point. But it was the quickest path to the swiftly moving pair. "You'll have to trust me. Or start on the stairs."

Muka clenched his jaw but strode forward. "How?"

"Climb onto the rail and raise your hands into the air; I'll catch on and we'll swing around to cut them off." Never dumped his pack, turned and ran for the rail a little further on, leaping up onto it and launching himself into the air with a shout. He pumped his wings and climbed, banking sharply so he could approach Muka, who balanced easily on the rail.

Their hands met with a slap, Muka's grip like iron.

Never winced but gripped back as they wheeled over buildings, heading for the end of the quiet street the two figures had used. It was harder to keep a comfortable height with Muka but he managed, even as he swooped a little low over one of the buildings, Muka lifting his legs.

Their targets were still running along the path as Never beat his wings, slowing their descent significantly where they neared an intersection. "This might be rough," he told Muka.

"Worry not."

The man released his hold.

Never glanced behind. Muka hit the ground in a roll, leaping to his feet as he drew his tyrant. Good. On Never flew, bearing down on the two figures. The taller of the pair pulled the smaller shape into a back street and Never angled his wings, slipping after.

Shouts followed him, cries of shock or warning he couldn't be sure, but he struck the paving stones and charged, using his momentum to close with the fleeing shapes as they burst into an open square lit by burning torches.

Never clenched his fists; the empty square and the lights were a bad sign. Had he made a mistake?

The robed figures stopped, then spun. Their hoods were raised, but the smaller of the two stood a little away from her companion, body seeming tensed, even obscured by the folds of the robe. The other stood calmly, blade sheathed.

"Let her go and I let you go," Never said.

The smaller one – the woman, he was sure of it – turned to the man. His hood creased in a nod and she ran forward. Never raised a hand. "Slowly."

But she ran on.

"Please, Ayuni."

Even as he called the words, they seemed foolish.

And then her hood fell back, revealing a topknot of dark hair, shaven high, and fierce eyes – she was Kiymako. He'd taken the bait.

The young woman drew a pair of knives.

Never leapt back.

She slashed with her blade, but he was already gone, using his wings to climb up out of reach. The woman spun, tossing a knife in one motion. Never tilted his wings and the blade whistled past. He flung his own knife down. It lodged in her leg. She stumbled back with a curse. Never dropped down before his enemy, catching a wrist then backhanding her with his birch hand.

She crumpled to the ground.

He turned on the hooded man – pointing a finger. "This was a mistake, whoever you are."

The man pushed his hood back, revealing a wrinkled face and white hair threaded with silver beads.

Hiruso.

"I did underestimate you, Never, last of the Amouni." The monk drew his *sisan*.

"We both know I am not the last," Never spat.

Now he smiled. "Last to roam free, then."

Never drew both knives, cutting into his hand, digging a little deep. But the pain was fleeting, his anger burnt it away as a globe of crimson-fire burst free. He flared it as he charged – letting a burst fly at the man's chest.

Hiruso lifted his blade and spun... dancing aside, the movement seeming slow and graceful yet the crimson fire flew into the dark, missing by a dozen feet. The old monk was already upon Never, swinging his blade down in a vicious arc.

How did he move so quickly?

Never rolled.

Something hot sliced into his back, running along one of his wings. He found his feet and Hiruso was before him once more, fist flying out to strike Never in the chest. Air boomed with the blow and Never flew across the stones. Bone cracked as he landed, sliding to a halt, struggling to breathe. Pain flared all through his chest and back – one of his wings was likely broken.

Again, Brother Hiruso stepped close, a graceful move that seemed almost languid as it covered the distance between them within the blink of an eye, his limbs seeming to blur. Never flared his crimson-fire in a wild spray. The monk lifted the sleeve of his robe. The fabric hissed and burned but when his arm dropped, he was unharmed.

"How young you are, Amouni. Did your father teach you nothing?"

He lifted his blade and swung.

Sparks flashed.

A second tyrant blocked the first – Muka stood over him, blade extended. His expression was one of extreme effort and his cheek bore a thin cut, his forearms several more where they'd slipped free from the sleeve of his robe.

Hiruso stepped back. "So this is the mighty Mukatagami, Sword of Stone?"

"Never, you can still catch her wagon." Muka did not take his eyes from the old monk.

Never hauled himself away, still struggling to take in

air. Muka attacked, his own movements possessing the same strange fluidity of Brother Hiruso. Their swords met once more and Hiruso pushed Muka back. They spun and twisted, flashing and cutting, their blades trailing fire as the torchlight reflected and then failed to keep up with the combatants.

But Muka was taking more cuts than Hiruso. And he was slower, it seemed. He leapt over a spinning slash, landing close, whirling so that his elbow cracked into Hiruso's face.

The monk fell back but answered with a blow of his own – only he knelt to drive his fist into the ground. Stone and earth exploded around Muka. He was flung to the ground, his blade clattering away.

"Not as good as your master, I see." Brother Hiruso strode forward, stopping before the dazed Muka. He lifted his weapon high.

Never flung one of his knives as Hiruso whipped his sword downwards.

The dagger flew across the square. The monk turned his head, slightly, but his sword plunged into Muka. Blood spurted.

Never roared, even as his throw struck the monk square in the back.

Brother Hiruso hissed as he spun – then stopped. His gaze shifted to a point beyond Never and he drew his hood, covering his face. "You have a chance to leave Kiymako, Never. Take it, for she is ours and you must realise you cannot possibly best me."

The old monk strode toward the opposite end of the square. When he reached the wall he leapt up, his movements once more becoming difficult to trace with the eye, and then he was gone.

Never hauled himself to his feet and staggered to Muka's side.

A deep wound in the man's chest still pumped blood. Hiruso's strike had missed the man's heart but Muka's eyes were already glazing as he laboured to cling to life. Never's own blood was stirring and he closed his fist and fought his curse, controlling his blood's thirst.

"What happened here?" a voice cried.

A crowd had formed in the square. Half stared in horror at his wings, the other at Muka, covered in blood. Never shouted at them. "Find a healer. And Niswan the seamstress," he added. The nearest man flinched, but ran off. Others drew closer, offering help. A woman was calling for a monk but it was all noise to Never.

He had to save Muka. But how, Gods, how?

For all his Amouni powers he was useless. All his blood could do was kill and destroy... and yet, there was a chance. If he took a dire risk, there was hope because there was one thing his blood could do better now, ever since it had been mixed with the sap of the Bleak Man's tree.

Never turned away from the fading Muka with a grunt, the movement sending lances of pain down his wing, and cut into his hand once more. Blood pooled and he snapped at the nearest onlooker. "Help me!"

The man jumped forward. "How?"

"Hold out your hands, quickly."

He did as instructed. Never poured the blood into the fellow's palm, glaring at him when the man started to tremble. "Place this over his wound – now."

"But –"

"Do it!"

The man sprang into action, crashing to his knees beside Muka and placing his bloody hands over the wound. He swallowed as he did so, then fell back. Never jammed his bleeding hand beneath his arm and leant over Muka.

"Please, Pacela," he whispered in Marlosi.

There.

The man's breathing was growing stronger already! Even Muka's eyes started to regain focus. An arm twitched and soon after, his eyes slowly closed. His breathing continued, easy breaths, as if the man simply slept and did not have an open wound in his chest – yet the gaping hole remained. Was it enough?

And more, what consequences would wait for Muka if he survived, now that he'd had Amouni blood forced into his body?

"Where are the healers?" Never said, his voice rasping.

"On their way, Lord," a voice replied, awe clear.

He let his chin slump onto his chest, closing his own eyes a moment as weariness overcame his own pain. "Good. Tell them to hurry."

Chapter 16

In the bright lamplight, Niswan glared at him from where she leant over a garment of blue and green silk in her workshop. "He still hasn't woken, has he?" A variety of pins and needles, along with a pair of small scissors were pinned to her apron.

"No." He rolled his shoulders to ease some discomfort. His own healing was doing its job well enough, but he wouldn't be flying anywhere soon, he knew that much. Forcing his wings to fold and retract had been blinding – but once he'd managed it the pain seemed to ease, as if they would heal better within. The same Amouni magic that allowed them to somehow fit within his body was hopefully helping his already accelerated healing. "But he is getting better, the wound is smaller."

Tears built, and she shook her head as if to stop them. "I told you..."

"He will wake, I am sure of it." Never wasn't sure yet – but he was growing more confident. A different concern lingered with the doubt. Would Muka be the same when he did?

"He had better."

"He's like family, isn't he?"

She nodded but did not elaborate. Instead, she tossed a spindle of green thread to the table and slumped onto her stool. "It is not safe for you here anymore, Never. Word has already spread throughout the city about the winged man. You cannot hide on the roof every time the monks visit – and they will return and be more thorough."

"I know," he said. "Will you be safe?"

"I can handle them – they won't do anything to me, the temple relies on me for more than Ayuni's dress."

"You sure about that?"

"I am."

"What about Muka?"

"They'll want to interview him if... when he wakes. He'll decide whether he wants to speak with them."

"Maybe I should stay a little longer, just in case."

"Don't be a fool; you'll only bring the wrong attention – and I've had enough of that for the rest of my damn life."

She was probably right. "Forgive me for that, and please thank Muka when he recovers. He saved me from Hiruso." The deadly monk was another reason to leave – if Brother Hiruso came looking, Never had to lead the menace away from Niswan and Muka.

Niswan nodded. "Take whatever you need from the pantry. And if you reach Mondami, seek Pinshe in the Blue Feather. He owes me a favour."

"And now I owe you one, Niswan."

"Then you'd better survive; I want to call it in."

He smiled but it faded. "There's something else."

"It had better not be more bad news."

"I don't think so." Would Cog or Andramir have felt that what Snow had done to them was troubling? Perhaps Cog, who'd always had a sliver of Amouni heritage. But Andramir had remained adamantly proud of the changes. What would Muka think if he woke and *knew* something had changed within him? There was no reason to believe Never had changed the man significantly. If anything, surely, Muka might now heal a little quicker, after taking on a comparatively small amount of Never's blood.

"Never?"

"Sorry. Just tell him – Muka – that my blood might have changed him. He might heal swiftly now. I can't be sure."

"So be it, Never. If you did save him, it will be worth it. Now hurry."

Never collected a new pack – the third in a short span of time, and filled it with provisions, water and a blanket taken from one of Niswan's shelves. She'd also given him a small salve of healing balm that smelt vaguely of lavender, and a pair of cheap daggers. Their balance was not fit for throwing but they were sharp, and it brought his total back up to comfortable levels. On his way from the kitchen he paused to offer her one more smile, and then he was striding along the passage leading to her back door.

He raised his hood before leaving; passing through the small square and heading along a narrow side street before entering the main thoroughfare where the flow of people and small carts created a hum uncommon to early morning, but it seemed harvest was in full swing.

But Never did not stay on the thoroughfare long, instead crossing to another shadowed side street, moving steadily north. He soon came across a busy market. Slipping through would allow him to avoid the Tower of the Heavens and the scene of his... encounter with Brother Hiruso. Even to himself, Never couldn't call it a fight or a contest – the monk had not even broken a sweat.

Voices called to him as he strode through the press of people, offering meat, silk, spice or jewellery but he did not turn his head or slow until a press of people arguing over prices forced him to find a new path. Never muttered a curse and backtracked a little, finding himself having to squeeze between a stall and a cart loaded with colourful vegetables.

"You there, traveller." A woman in a soft blue robe stepped before him.

"Forgive me, I am late," Never said as he stepped around her.

She caught his tunic. "The monks are looking for you, aren't they?"

He broke her grasp and shoved his way through the crowd. Shouts rose behind him; the woman's screeches for help mixed with complaints and swearing. Never did not turn back, he pushed on, finally breaking free and skidding into an empty alley where he paused to catch his breath.

There was no sound of footsteps following, but the swell of voices did seem to be growing. Would they form a search party? Either way, someone would be heading for a temple by now. Maybe even the Divine Temple, which wouldn't bode well for the Northern Gate – a problem he hadn't quite solved yet. A bluff was unlikely. Waiting until nightfall and flying... his wings might not hold. And staying hidden so long might not be possible.

Which left force or subterfuge.

And the longer he delayed, the further Ayuni was taken

from Takbisu.

"You seem concerned, friend."

Never spun.

A heavyset man approached from nearby; perhaps he'd left one of the buildings? His tunic was patched, and he wore a short sword but did not draw it. When he neared, a tattoo... no, a *brand* on his cheek became clear. This was nothing Hanael had mentioned.

"Just catching my breath," he said.

The fellow paused, then smiled, the expression quite unsavoury. "That's a fine accent you have there."

"A pleasure to have brought you such joy," Never said.

"Let me help you," the man said. "For a price, I can sneak you from the city."

"Can you now?"

His smile did not falter. "You can trust me, friend. I'd like nothing more than to thwart every last monk in that temple. Think about it, why would *I* of all people turn you over to those prying bastards."

"You?"

"Right." He gestured to the twin slashes branded on his cheek. "Understand yet?"

Never raised an eyebrow. "I could guess that you didn't earn that brand for being an upstanding citizen but beyond that, I still don't know if I can trust you, *friend*."

"Well said. Call me Unai...?"

"Never."

He tilted his head to the side. "Never, huh? That's an odd name, even for a Marlosi."

"I'm pretty odd, even for a Marlosi."

Unai chuckled. "Well, now that introductions are out of

the way let's get down to it. I let you through the tunnel beneath the walls for a fair price or you can try your luck at the lake. You might be able to steal a boat, I don't know."

Never shook his head. "Too slow, I need to go north. What's your price?"

"Fifty gold crescents."

"I have a blanket."

Unai folded his arms. "What?"

"Do I look like I have any money?"

"Then what do you have, Never? I'm going to need something if I'm going to help you."

"What if someone else could vouch for me?"

"It would have to be someone impressive."

Never grinned. "How about Mukatagami, Sword of Stone?"

"Ha. You do not know Mukatagami."

"I saved his life last night – why don't you ask around? I'm guessing you've already heard about the fight near the Divine Temple?"

"That I have." He considered Never a moment. "New deal. You meet me before the Many Hands Inn and if your story's true, I'll take you through the tunnel myself."

"Agreed."

Unai turned, striding away. "And don't rush."

Never moved to the mouth of the alley and paused. It was still quiet enough that few people were about here. He slipped into the street and started north once more, bypassing larger groups and once, when a pair of monks appeared ahead, he calmly turned down the nearest street – then sprinted the moment he was out of sight.

When he finally came across the Many Hands Inn, he

saw the rotund figure of Unai leaning against the wall. The man marked Never, then stepped inside without hailing him. Never followed. Cheer and chatter filled a bright common room, servers racing around the tables, but Unai had not taken a seat.

He was holding a door open at the end of a long corridor. Never quickened his step and Unai led him through a store room, shouting from the kitchen audible as the man began moving crates and sacks of rice and wheat.

"Going to help me then?" he asked.

Never accepted a bag of wheat. "Sounds like you believe me."

He grunted as he set his load down, gesturing to the floor. A heavy steel ring was half uncovered. "Right. You saved Muka, so you pass for free – but only if you lend a hand."

Never helped the man finish clearing the stores then lifted the hatch. Darkness below, ladder rungs visible. Not so dissimilar to when he'd had to escape Isacina. How long ago that seemed now.

"I'll lead," Unai said from where he was checking over a lantern. "This won't take long. You'll get out in the fields, parallel with the north highway."

"Perfect."

"Follow me, then." Unai started down the ladder and Never gave him some room before joining the descent. The ladder soon ended, and he found himself in a dusty tunnel, wide enough for one and a half men only. Unai was already moving.

They travelled in silence – save for Unai's cursing when he encountered a few spider webs. Never didn't offer to trade positions. Time wore on, but a growing excitement fuelled his steps. He was getting closer now; he knew where Ayuni was, he just had to catch up.

And yet, doubt lingered. Brother Hiruso's power was unfathomable... and more, he'd seemed to possess some knowledge about Father. It *could* have been an assumption on the monk's part. But what if it wasn't? Hiruso was old enough to have been an important part of the temple when Ayuni was abandoned and even now, he was keeping her prisoner.

Using her blood for something.

Was *that* the source of his power? Possible, but his abilities seemed unlike anything Never had encountered when it came to the Amouni – more likely it was the *lunai* Hanael mentioned. Still, it would be foolish to rule out the possibility.

Worse would be if Father had somehow helped or approved of the temple's actions. Not unbelievable but disturbing nonetheless.

"Unai, what do you know about Brother Hiruso?"

"I know that it's best to keep out of his way."

"But nothing about his *lunai*?"

The man shook his head. "Temple secrets, friend."

"Of course." Never smothered a sigh as he walked on.

Chapter 17

Never crouched at the edge of the rice fields – a long, flat wetland that stretched either side of the northern highway, stepping down toward lower ground in verdant green tiers. The road was broad, well-maintained, wide enough for two wagons to pass. It stood empty now, but the fields were dotted with farmers. Not so many either, perhaps they were taking a mid-morning break.

In any event, he had to make up for a lot of lost time. His legs were ready, even if his wings were not. Unai was already gone, all that was left was for Never to make his move. He broke into a crouching run, leaving the overgrown opening in the ground to cross the hard earth and join the road, where he straightened into a jog.

The wagon and its heavy steel load would not have been making great time – and hopefully they'd stopped for the night the previous evening. Still, he'd have his work cut out for him.

He alternated between jogging and walking until noon, when he leant against a stunted tree to drink and eat from

The Phoenix of Kiymako

the supplies Niswan provided. No sign of the wagon yet, but once his wings healed he'd make up for lost time.

Never started out once more; approaching a sharp bend in the road. A single traveller approached, dragging something on a sled. Never kept a hand near a dagger as he drew near but the fellow simply nodded as he passed, neatly bundled bags of some manner of foodstuffs tied to his sling.

Beyond the bend, Never slowed. The rice fields still stretched around the road but the path dipped before it climbed up again and within the depression, set off the highway, was a scene of wreckage – blackened debris covered the earth, ravaging even the edges of the wet crops. A mighty lightning strike?

Two warrior monks stood before the scene, hands on their hilts.

Beyond them, a line of charred bodies had been arranged. Six or seven... Never forced himself to walk casually. The monks had noticed him and would be watching as he passed, yet his whole body seemed to hum with tension.

Six or seven guards?

Ayuni...

The human remains were little more than shrivelled limbs, features reduced to a shiny black. Not too far away, a slagheap of melted steel covered the ground and beyond that in turn, twin lumps of black. Flies hovered and the cloying scent of burnt flesh clung to the air.

The bodies were of a size, as best he could tell.

Ayuni did not appear to be one of them – yet what had happened here?

"Traveller, where are you headed?"

One of the monks was waving for him to leave the road.

The distance was hardly so great that the man wouldn't soon notice the fact that Never was not Kiymako.

"Your way," Never said as he charged.

The man stumbled back half a step before tearing his *sisan* free. Never had already flung one of his blades, his favourite with the triangular patterns, and it thudded into the man's thigh. He fell aside as Never sidestepped to slash at the second warrior, who deflected his blow with her sword. She followed with her own attack, chopping down from left and right as he dodged.

Never tried to slip inside her guard but she leapt back.

He glanced back to the man, who was circling, sword ready as he limped.

"No time for this," Never muttered. He sliced into the back of his hand, letting a globe of crimson-fire build. It engulfed his entire forearm as he whirled, spraying searing blood at the wounded man. The monk dived but his injured leg failed him; flames tore across his body. He crashed to the burnt earth, screaming.

The other monk hissed, her eyes wide. But she did not attack. Instead, she spun and sprinted away, disappearing down the highway as Never watched. He approached the other warrior, bending to jerk his blade free. The man did not respond – already dead. "You were part of this," he told the corpse, then strode to the great heap of melted steel.

It seemed to have burst out in a spray, like a deadly flower opening.

As if something within had burnt its way free... he frowned. Could Ayuni have been responsible? Did she even know how to use crimson-fire? There was a chance it was something else entirely. He paced. Too many questions – the most alarming of which being, if she had freed herself, and it was the crimson-fire, just how much blood had it cost?

Yet any doubts he had about her identity were falling away swiftly now.

It was obvious too, that she was in danger.

He started a circuit of the area, splashing into the nearest field – a line of blackened rice. Never hopped onto the earthen barrier and ran, following the rows of ruined grasses until he reached a pair of bodies. One hung over the barrier, legs dangling, the other lay motionless in the crop. The man in the water possessed no hands – they'd been burnt to stubs, and the other monk was headless. Ash floated in the water.

Never ran on.

The tier curved around a hillside but halfway along, the path veered sharply across the paddy. A third corpse waited for him there, face-down in the rice. By the level of burns, something similar to the bodies near the road, the monk had died a horrible death. Yet he'd obviously expressed some level of bravery, or madness, to have pursued his charge considering he would have seen what happened to his fellows.

Or perhaps it was fear – fear of what Brother Hiruso would do, should he fail.

The trail led toward the hillside. Never leapt over the body and increased his pace, quickly drawing closer to the hill, where he splashed to a halt.

The trail of ashes led directly to the wall of earth and grass but did not stop. It simply continued, tunnelling through as if some mighty ball of fire had pummelled its way into the very hill.

Chapter 18

Never approached the opening.

Slowly.

Soot-scarred earth revealed only darkness, a single spec of ash fluttering down even as he watched. Using crimson-fire to burn through earth was not all that surprising, considering Snow had used it to blast through the Temple of Jyan's roof in City-Sedrin.

What gave Never pause was the blind fury of what he'd witnessed so far. He lifted his birch hand, the one that had essentially grown back after Snow had melted it down to the bone. There was a real chance she'd hurt him if he wasn't careful.

He stepped within. "Ayuni?"

Gods, if he was wrong... if he'd come so far only to have been mistaken, his blood, his belief, his damnable hope, all of it wrong, what was he supposed to do then? But that was foolish, surely, after seeing what had happened to the guards?

No-one answered his call.

Light from the opening extended a little way in and then became shadow only. He called again, louder. The dark swallowed his voice. He let a small globe of fire grow in his hands, enough to cast light. The tunnel walls were straight, a pure cut.

It extended some distance. His lungs began to swell and tighten as he walked – damn it, he was holding his breath. He exhaled and quickened his step.

How deep was it going to... he stopped, both the question and his feet.

A shape lay huddled against the earthen wall.

"Ayuni?"

It stirred at the sound of his voice. He flared the fire – only a little – and moved closer. A young woman wearing a torn silken dress, twin to that which Niswan had made, was blinking at the light, raising a shaking hand.

The girl from Isansho Shika's painting, only older now. Her features were Kiymako yet the Marlosi – and Amouni – heritage was clear.

Ayuni, his sister.

Relief covered her face. "She said you would come one day."

Never swallowed, unsure of his next words.

She hauled herself into an upright position, revealing another tear in her garment, grazed skin beneath, but she smiled and gestured for him to come closer.

He tried to speak, fighting the words a moment. "You know me?" he finally asked. How could... it didn't matter now. He knelt beside her, the stirrings of joy buried deep beneath his worry. Who knew how quickly pursuit could be organised? Would she be able to walk? "We have to leave.

Are you hurt?" Up close, fading bruises on her cheek and neck were visible and when she nodded, reaching out to take his free hand, old scars gleamed pink in the light.

He clenched his jaw. Bastards! Just how many years had they been draining her blood? At least his scars were his own choice.

"Yes. But I'll recover," Ayuni said.

Never pushed aside a thousand questions. There'd be a better time – they had to escape. But one question could not be denied. "Who told you I would come?"

"My mother. We have to find her... Brother..." she said, finishing hesitantly.

Another hundred questions sprang to mind but he set them aside too. "It's Never."

She smiled at him. "Never? That's truly your name?"

He helped her stand and she winced. "I bet you won't forget it, will you?" he said as they started toward the tunnel's opening. "We need somewhere we can hide from Hiruso's men."

"There are abandoned farmhouses to the west – we've taken refuge there during storms before. We'd reach one before nightfall I think."

"Good enough for now," he said, pausing at the mouth of the cave to scan the paddies. No monks prowled about, no field-workers either. Clouds were passing over the afternoon sun. He led her out and they splashed their way to the nearest barrier, then followed it west. Beneath them in the lower tiers, the paddies were filled with workers bent over the harvest, with more climbing up toward the upper levels.

"They'll talk, won't they," Never said.

"Some gladly, some to save themselves."

"Then we won't be able to stay long."

Ayuni nodded beside him as she jogged along. She was keeping pace easily enough – there was no sign of the massive blood loss she must have sustained after her escape. Yet another mystery he had to set aside for the time being.

They spoke little as they fled, using narrow roads between the fields, saving their breath for running. Ayuni directed him as they left the highway further and further behind, the sun toppling down toward the horizon before they came across an abandoned farmhouse. The building was sinking into the very earth where it presided over a weed-choked field, windows darkened – another home rested further away, it too stood in a barren field. How long since people had abandoned the land?

The front door lay rotting across the entryway, a lizard darting into the shadows when they neared. Inside, those shadows were made deeper by occasional shafts of light from the broken roof.

The first room was bare of all but dirt. Another still bore a table and a single chair. He offered it to Ayuni, then dumped his pack on the table. Then he handed her water, which she accepted, and moved to lean against the doorframe. From his vantage point, if he turned his head, he could see the fields through the empty window and front door but that only covered one approach.

Silence stretched between them and he found himself unsure of what to say – she was probably too exhausted to deal with a barrage of questions from him in any event. Somehow, it'd been easier when they were actually fleeing. Their words had been limited to escape.

"Mother said you would be like him but also nothing

like him," she said, almost blurting the words out, as if the quiet had begun to make her uneasy too. She looked down. "Forgive me."

"Our father?"

"Yes." A look of sadness entered her dark eyes – and perhaps bitterness too. Which was entirely understandable.

"I take no offense," he said quickly, hoping to reassure her. "I don't suppose he visited you many times?"

She shrugged. "Twice."

Never considered his next question. As before, there were so many to choose from but if he was being honest with himself, hearing about Father failing yet another of his children wasn't high up on his list of moments to anticipate.

"You're thinking about the men and women back there, aren't you?" she asked. She continued before he could reply. "I hadn't planned it... to kill them, I mean. But I used the Fire of Heaven. You probably know it too. Do you call it that?"

"No, but I doubt there is a single name for it only."

A haunted expression became somewhat lighter, as though she'd gladly pushed aside some shame perhaps. "I've wanted to ask you for the longest time, ever since I was a child. Isn't that silly of me?"

"No, not really."

"Well, that and so many things, I suppose. Mother said I have another brother – is he travelling with you? Can we meet him here? Or would we have to leave Kiymako? I'd love to see the golden plains of Marlosi."

Never opened his mouth to reply but couldn't manage. An image of he and Snow teaching Ayuni, of laughing and smiling together sliced into him like the coldest of blades.

Not just its impossibility but the weight of his sudden desire for something that could never come to pass – for something he hadn't quite realised he'd even desired before this moment.

"Oh, I'm sorry."

He shook his head. "No, don't be. He... died some time ago."

She stood and crossed the room, hesitating before reaching out to take his hand. Her eyes widened slightly as she noticed his own scars. When she looked up, her gaze was a mix of earnestness and fierceness. "At least I found you."

"The Gods must have had a hand in that," Never said. "I've been floundering since I arrived, and it looks like you saved yourself back there."

"I'm not so sure. Mother told me I'd be able to use the Fire of Heaven one day, but I didn't know it was so powerful." She drew in a shuddering breath. "Brother Hiruso had been to see me in Takbisu and I don't know... I just couldn't bear to have them cut into me yet again. It was so sudden, like a damn had built up and burst. Every mile in that... prison... I grew madder and madder and suddenly I knew how to call the fire. Does that make sense?"

"I think so. I certainly wasn't taught everything I know. Some things simply seem to lie within my blood."

"I see. So... can it be controlled?"

"It can."

She gave a sigh of relief. "Well, when I called... such a roaring came with it, fire was everywhere. When I could see again I had melted everything. And the bodies were... I couldn't recognise them anymore."

"But others chased you."

"Yes. I don't know what I was doing after. I... I think I was hoping someone had survived. There was one guard, Chani. He'd been so kind. I thought maybe I could save him. It's a stupid thing to say, I know. And I don't know how long I stared at his body before the others came – but that's when I ran."

"And when they caught you?"

"I burned them without exactly meaning to." Tears built in her eyes. "I don't want it to be like this; I want to *help* people."

The impulse to put an arm around Ayuni rose but he was still a stranger to her – she might not welcome it, yet he couldn't just stand there like a lump either. He took her by the shoulders. "I know. I felt the same for the longest time about my blood. I still feel the same – it doesn't get much better, but you can live with it."

She laughed, sniffing and wiping at her eyes. "I didn't want you to lie, Never, but you know you can soften the blow a little."

"Next time, I promise."

Chapter 19

They ate fruit and flatbread as darkness fell, and again Never kept watch on the doorway, listening too, but it seemed there was at least enough time to finish their meal before leaving once more. If pursuit was to come, even aided by the field-workers, it would have to actually *reach* the site of Ayuni's escape before locating and then following their trail.

"So where is your mother?" Never asked.

"In the Cesanha Mountains," she said. Ayuni was much calmer now but the troubled look had not totally left her eyes.

Never raised an eyebrow as he took a drink of water. "Isn't that halfway across Kiymako? She must have mighty lungs to tell you I was coming from there."

She laughed, and the welcome sound eased his own worry. "No. She told me when I was very young, before Father came to take me away."

"Ah. When was that?"

"I was five, I think. It's been nearly twelve years at the end of this summer, of being carted from temple to temple so they could drain me for their salves."

Never lowered his flask. "They use your blood for healing?"

She nodded. "The monks mix it with regular medicine and use it to save those who cannot be healed by regular means, and sometimes themselves. Part of me is glad that my blood can help people..."

"You're not something for them to harvest, Ayuni," he said, a little more sharply than he'd intended.

But she only nodded.

Never found himself pacing again. Once more, Father had revealed new depths of his depravity. Was there no limit to how far the man could sink? "Is that why he left you at the temple?"

"He only told me I would be safe there, and that the monks would protect me," she said. "And that he would return soon."

"A lie I'm sure he spoke to many."

"To you?" she asked.

"Not that I remember... but certainly to my mother," he said. "But I'm sorry to have led the conversation to him. Tell me more of your mother and how you think we can reach her. Is she an Isansho or can she help us escape Brother Hiruso somehow?"

"I think she can, yes. But in my mind, she was always more humble than any overseer. If we can reach the mountains, I would love for you to meet her, Never."

"And I her." He glanced into the darkness beyond the farmstead. The moon would be rising soon, their best chance to travel swiftly. Now that he'd actually found Ayuni, he had to protect her and if that meant travelling halfway across

Kiymako then he'd do just that. "Do you have any ideas of how we're going to reach the mountains?"

"I didn't think about it when I called the fire. I simply ran – I'm sorry."

"Don't be, we'll figure something out. We can start with the cover of darkness." She probably didn't know the countryside too well, if she'd been confined to temples or a steel cage most of her life, but there was still Niswan's friend Pinshe in the Blue Feather. Even if heading to the capital would be a great risk, there was at least one person who might be able to help.

And visiting Mondami wouldn't be much of a detour at all, since both it and the mountain range lay to the east of Takbisu.

Still, was it too great a risk?

Before finding Ayuni, he hardly had a plan of his own for what would happen *after*. He'd simply needed her to exist. But now he might have a chance at more – he'd found a family member who needed him. And perhaps someone who would understand him, who might see the world like he did. Who might become the sibling Snow should have been.

And Never would protect her no matter what they faced.

"Never? Is something wrong?"

He sighed. "I'm trying to think of someone who might be able to help us. I have a name but they're in the capital. I'm not thrilled about travelling closer to Brother Hiruso."

"I know perhaps two monks in all the temples who I would trust. One resides in the capital and the other in Yalinamo. I think we need a disguise."

"Any ideas?"

"How about a Lady and her Bodyguard?"

"Well, it's not far from the truth at all but I still don't think I'll ever pass for Kiymako," he said with a smile.

"The very rich have been known to employ foreign blades. People will assume you're a holdover from before the sealing of the harbour."

"All right, that might do for most people, but the monks will be looking for me specifically – and you too."

"Then we need to act the part," she said. Her voice grew hard with resolve. "And put a stop to any who see through."

"Agreed," he said. Obviously she didn't want to be recaptured and he'd burn every damn monk to the ground before he let them take her. "And I can't think of anything else so let's try it. But we're still going to need help with this. I know someone but we have to head back to Takbisu City."

"Are you sure?"

He nodded. "More and more. Hiruso's men will be focusing their search *beyond* the point of your escape. They'll assume that neither of us would be stupid enough to return to a densely populated place like Takbisu."

She hesitated. "But thanks to you, we are?"

"I know. But they don't know that," he said with a grin. "So, all we have to do is slip inside and let Niswan look after us."

Ayuni blinked, a hand reaching up to touch the silk at her throat. "Niswan the Seamstress?"

A voice spoke from the darkness. "Yes, but I'd rather we left her out of it this time."

Never spun, dagger in hand but the voice was familiar. A large shape blocked the light. "Muka?"

"It is." He entered, footfalls soft. When he reached their

room, he inclined his head to Ayuni. "Lady. I am relieved to see you well." He was sweating but moved easily enough; he still bore a tyrant and pack with little to suggest he'd recently been mortally stricken.

Ayuni stood, offering him her chair. "Please, you look exhausted."

"I fear we cannot afford to rest until we find a safer place to do so."

Never introduced Muka to Ayuni properly before turning back to the warrior. "You've seen searchers?"

"None, but they will be heading this way sooner or later. And if I could follow the traces of spent *lunai*, believe others will be able."

Never met the man's gaze. "Niswan didn't let you follow us, did she?"

"I do not need a nursemaid."

"That's not why she's worried –"

"I meant you, Never," he said with a faint smile. "Understand, I have come here to fulfil not only my word as I gave it to Wanatek, but my debt to you. I owe you my life."

Never shook his head. "You're too forgiving; it was my idiocy that landed us in that mess with Hiruso in the first place."

"You must accept me if you are to help your sister."

"And you have to tell us if you need to rest. I saw what he did, Muka. Even with my blood, you must need more time to heal."

"A warrior heals through action."

"A lovely thought but I'm not carrying you if you collapse," Never said.

Again, his smile was slight. "That is fair."

Chapter 20

Muka led them along the road, heading into the first blush of sunrise.

It had taken the rest of the night to wind their way down the tiers and start east across level grassland toward the village of Osa, which was only half a day south of Mondami. There, Muka was sure, was a woman who could help them with a better disguise. "She is a *rudama*," he'd said, explaining that it meant 'sorceress' when Never asked.

Now they crouched within a stand of trees, looking down upon a guard post in the distance, two men stationed before a low, wooden barrier. One man looked to be carrying a bow, but it was hard to tell in the poor light.

"This is not the only road heading toward Osa but it is the most direct," Muka explained.

"I can distract them," Ayuni said.

"What do you have in mind?" Never asked.

"Fire."

Never frowned; the memory of her tearful expression from earlier still vivid. "If we're planning on burning them, let me."

"No. I mean, that stand of trees off to the right. I think I can start a fire there."

Muka was nodding. "Let's try it; we can circle around from—"

"No, Muka. I think we might be close enough," she said, though her expression was one of doubt. She knelt and closed her eyes. Next, Ayuni raised her hands, palms open before her. She cupped them and after a moment, a dancing flame of green and blue appeared. Never blinked. No knife, no blood, no crimson flame – just how different was what she called the Fire of Heaven? More *lunai* power? Perhaps Muka would know.

Ayuni opened her eyes, shifting to face the trees. She drew in a deep breath and exhaled. The flame bent toward the distant trees and then flickered out. Ayuni stood with a satisfied smile. "I didn't know if I'd be able to do that."

A moment later, grey smoke began to billow forth from the stand.

The guards didn't react at first; not until an orange glow appeared. It was vivid against the shadowy stand of trees and the still lightening morning. Never turned back to the guards – one of which was now standing quite straight. After what appeared to be a short argument, he grabbed his fellow and started toward the growing blaze.

"Let's hurry," Ayuni said.

Once more, Muka led them along the hard-packed dirt of the road, moving swiftly. Between watching their surroundings and looking out for Ayuni, Never had done his best to keep an eye on Muka too, but the man was not showing any signs of slowing. He was still sweating, and his movement wasn't totally free, particularly when it came to twisting his torso, but he was healing remarkably well. Even for someone who had Amouni blood applied directly to a wound... his own *lunai* at work?

And then there was Ayuni's Fire of Heaven. It wasn't so dissimilar to crimson-fire but nor was it the same. Had Father... done something to her? The monks? Ayuni didn't seem to know all that much about it herself. Was her mother guiding her somehow? Just who had Father chosen as part of his dark plan to propagate Amouni children? A Kiymako sorceress?

The guard post slipped by and they continued on toward Osa.

"Should I put it out?" Ayuni sounded concerned.

"Best to let them," Never replied. "We can't afford to turn back."

The sun had well-and-truly risen by the time they reached Osa. The village ran along the banks of a stream, dozens of buildings surrounded by more green rice fields and in places, crops of tomato plants and other vegetables, too.

Few people were about; most were at work in the fields but those that remained watched them as they passed by, heading for a home set a little ways beyond the rest. Never kept his hood raised, hoping people would focus more on Muka. It seemed there was no temple at least.

"Let's hope she's home," Muka said when they reached the wooden door. A single large window bore closed curtains of clean white. He knocked and waited.

A voice called from within. "Who is it?"

"You can open up, Iri. It's Muka."

The scrape and thud of a bolt being drawn free followed, then the door swung open to reveal a young woman, probably a few years Ayuni's senior, wearing a heavy robe of fur, despite the warm sun. Yellow ribbons of varying shades had been woven throughout the fur and she wore a similar dyed headband.

"Muka, it's been a season already," she said with a warm smile. She pulled him inside. "Bring your friends."

Never let Ayuni enter first, then stepped into a single room – there were no dividing walls or curtains, just different furniture. One corner bore a neatly-made bed and the other a stove and two chairs around a table. Floor to ceiling shelving with a small stool before it, was packed with herbs, powders, vials and what appeared to be various parts of animal and insect, along with a collection of scrolls.

Muka handled the introductions and although Iri seemed surprised at Never, she grew wide-eyed at Ayuni. "You are the Princess in the Temple?"

Ayuni shook her head. "Just a prisoner, truly."

Never glanced at his sister – was she starting to sound like him? Surely he wasn't rubbing off on her so soon. Yet if so, it was a strangely comforting thought.

"Iri, we need your help," Muka said. "We have to be able to travel more freely. Can you do anything for Never, here?"

She scratched at her nose. "I think so. It won't be foolproof, but I have something. Let me find it." She moved to her shelves, stepping up onto the stool to reach for one of the higher shelves. She brought down a jar from beside a phoenix statue and removed a black fang. Next, she took an empty jar and filled it with water from a basin. To this, she stirred in silver powder and handed it to Muka. "Place this in the sun out back. It needs a bit of time."

He did as told.

"Thank you," Never told her. "What of Ayuni?"

"Few people outside the temple would recognise me, Never," she said. "It might be enough if I can change my clothing and hair." She reached up to take her dark hair into her hands.

"I might be able to help with that too," Iri said as Muka returned. "It'll take a little while, and it won't smell nice at first."

"I'm ready," Ayuni said.

The *rudama* collected a chair for Ayuni, placing it before the basin. Then she prepared another mixture, which she then applied to Ayuni's hair. A strong scent followed, and Never moved to the window when it became clear Ayuni wasn't going to be in any pain. "Can I open this?"

Iri nodded. "Just the window, leave the curtains."

He did as instructed, then looked to Muka. "I hate to ask, but how do you feel now?"

"Well enough."

"You're healing faster than I expected."

"That is a good thing, surely?"

Never chuckled. "I agree, but I didn't expect it – maybe it was how I administered the blood," he said. "But I wanted to warn you. Doing so might change you, and I'm not sure how yet."

He nodded. "Niswan told me. I would rather live changed than have died, you do not need to worry."

"Good," Never said. "I'd wondered if it had anything to do with your... other abilities. After all, everything else about you seemed pretty fast back there with Hiruso. You surprised me."

Iri had looked up from her work at mention of Hiruso,

brow furrowed. "Oh, you're not mixed up with him, are you?"

"Just until I repay my debt to Never," Muka said in a tone that was firm but not dismissive. Iri sighed but did not continue to question Muka, who turned back to Never. "Well, on the bridge I wasn't expecting you to have your own impressive abilities."

"But Brother Hiruso?"

"I'm still no-where near his match, that you saw."

"What is it? He could do things I've not encountered, and I've seen a lot of strange things over the years."

"It is an art, for mastery of the natural power within each man, each woman. Even children possess the power; it is no secret."

"I'll have to trust your word on that."

"My people call the art *lunai*, after the moon. The northern peoples of Kiymako call it *pho* and the Restless have their own word too. Usually, only members of the temple are given extensive training in the art."

"So both you and Wanatek?"

"Yes. Wanatek is my superior in the art but even he could not best Brother Hiruso alone – not now."

"If he stands in our way, together we will do what one cannot achieve," Ayuni said.

"I hope that is true, Lady."

Never nodded too, trying his best to offer some semblance of agreement, yet his doubts were not so easy to shake, despite the heartening show of unity.

Chapter 21

Iri handed him the now-dry black fang on a leather cord, which he tied around his neck and concealed within his clothing. "This charm is taken from the *yochan*, a mountain beast known for its ability to blend with its surroundings. For you, it will have a similar effect. I've made it so that those who look upon you will see what they expect to see. The charm suggests that you belong, for them."

Never touched it through his tunic. "This is a marvellous thing. How can I repay you?"

"Meeting Ayuni is its own reward," she said. "And before you try to argue, let me warn you of its limitations. Truly powerful monks like Brother Hiruso will see through it immediately, unlike regular people or common monks. But the further you are from the already familiar, the less potent the fang will be no matter who you face."

"And by that do you mean, the already familiar for Kiymako?"

"Yes. For instance, if you continue to dress as you are now, if you carry our weapons, eat our food, speak Kiyma and travel with Muka and Ayuni, you will seem Kiymako to those you meet. The sense of belonging will even extend to Muka and Ayuni if you are close."

"But if I were alone and say, speaking Marlosi, it would lose its potency?"

"In the right – or wrong – circumstances, even your accent may be enough to give you away, so keep everything I have told you in mind."

"I plan to stick close to Muka and Ayuni, believe me."

The rear door opened and Ayuni and Muka entered, their arms laden with pink wildflowers of some sort, which they'd gathered for their host. Ayuni's hair had changed from black to a golden brown. A sharp change, and hopefully enough to help confuse those who would be watching for them. Even Muka had made some effort to disguise himself, cutting and then shaving his greying hair close.

Iri wished them well, but took Muka's arm as they started out. "There's one more thing I want to ask you, Muka."

He nodded, then looked to Never. "I won't be far behind."

"Right."

Outside, Never and Ayuni started along the path that ran beside the stream. The sun was high overhead, a pleasant warmth, alleviated somewhat by a light breeze crossing the stream. Ahead, the fields were full of people heading back to eat, their robes a little shorter and more colourful here. Never kept his pace even – it was a fine time to test his charm.

As the people passed, few gave him a second look except to offer a greeting. Ayuni answered and he nodded with a smile.

Impressive indeed.

"Where are we headed next?" Never asked as the farmers thinned out.

"Still east. We'll eventually reach the Yalinamo Forest."

"Which lies beneath Cesanha?"

"Yes. I remember we stopped there on our journey down the mountain, it seemed such a large place to me as a child." She frowned. "My village was much smaller but I think there was still a Temple at least, or a large building in any event, only I don't think it was an inn. There was a river too."

"That's a start," Never said. "And once we climb the mountain and find the village, that's where we'll find your mother?"

She smiled up at Never and a sense of the familiar struck him. Her smile reminded him of Snow's – only Ayuni's smile was far more open. Somehow, despite the trials she'd been through her expression lacked Snow's bitterness. "I'm hoping she is still there, yes. And worry not; I believe I will be able to recall the way when the time comes."

"But you're not sure."

"For so long now I have lived in a world of steel and stone, peering through bars or temple windows. A world of blades and vials..."

Never met her gaze. "I will stop him if he comes for you."

"He will."

"Then let's put him to work," Never said. "He can cross the entire land and if he climbs the mountain, we'll cast him back down."

Thudding footsteps from their back trail neared. Never turned but it was only Muka approaching.

"Everything well?" Never asked.

"Yes. Iri simply wanted to give me something for the

pain," he said. "And a warning."

Never slowed. "Are we in danger here?"

"No. And she hesitated to worry us, for she is not certain. But as *rudama* she feels something stirring across the land."

"Something?"

"She fears the Three Hammers have been unleashed."

Ayuni gasped.

Never came to a halt. "That sounds unpleasant. And by your reaction, Ayuni, can I assume they're worse than Hiruso?"

"Perhaps not worse. But they are the temple's finest assassins. It is said they have not failed even once."

"I look forward to disappointing them," Never said.

Muka frowned. "Wanatek has long worried about their attention; he was sure we would be the Three's next target."

"Why would Brother Hiruso send them now?" Never asked. "Is he simply arrogant, assigning a task that is beneath him to some underlings?"

"I'm not sure," Ayuni said. "One of the monks who tended to me was talking of Brother Hiruso some weeks ago. He said the Master was busy searching for some great relic of power, that he was near to its discovery."

"More wonderful news," Never said.

Muka shrugged. "Whatever his purpose, we now have the Hammers to contend with. We must be extra watchful, for they will find us. It is only a matter of time."

"Can we stop them?" Never asked.

"Their *lunai* is strong, lesser than Hiruso but they are three."

"As are we. Your *lunai* is strong, I am Amouni and so is Ayuni. We can match them, can we not?" Never asked.

"If we are not surprised, I would hope so."

They continued on, heading for a crest where the road sloped up. Beyond, the eastern road stretched on through more farmland, but beyond it in turn, at the limits of his vision, a slight haze seemed to conceal a more barren terrain. The Cesanha Mountains were still too far to even catch a hint of, but they were closing slowly.

When evening fell, they'd reached a roadside inn surrounded by a large bamboo enclosure. Within, the snort and stamp of horses seemed to leap over the walls. "Somewhere for merchants to corral themselves?" Never asked.

Muka pointed to the stalls. "I see two different traders, one is on Temple business. See the Phoenix and the trunk of the red pine on the saddles? The trader is returning east, or on their way to the capital."

"Another opportunity to test our disguises then," Never said.

Muka nodded as he led them through the doors and into a busy common room. Few heads turned, though a group nearest the windows paid them some attention. "I spot two monks, though they are dressed more casually," Ayuni said as they took their own table.

"So far no alarm bells," Never said.

The conversation in the room seemed to centre around the condition of the roads and some 'commotion over at Takbisu' though no-one had the truth of it. Once they had drinks – a fruity wine – and meals placed before them, Never lowered his voice a little.

"Ayuni, I wanted to ask about your mother. And our father," he said after a moment of hesitation. On the surface,

Ayuni seemed at ease, seemed that she was dealing with her long imprisonment and sudden freedom well enough. But if she wasn't, and asking such questions was simply going to reopen old wounds, he'd just as soon keep his mouth shut.

"I'll tell you what I can, of course."

"Thank you." He sighed. How to explain his fear without alluding to Father's particular evil? "Ayuni, do you think we have any more siblings?"

She frowned. "Mother only mentioned two brothers as far as I remember."

"And did she explain anything of your heritage? As Amouni?"

"Yes. The supposedly mythical race that once ruled all the lands; their blood ran in your father's veins and now mine. He told me how important I was and how some would wish me harm; which is why he left me in the care of the Temple."

"Didn't he trust your mother?"

Ayuni shook her head, a look of sadness on her face. "I wish I knew. I seem to remember Mother arguing with Father on the day we left but more than that I see her smiling at me. Hear her tell me that she would see me again."

"Let's prove her right then," Never said. A promise was right behind the words but he left it unspoken this time. What if he *couldn't* deliver? For all his Amouni blood, Brother Hiruso had certainly wiped the stones with him. And now, he had the Hammers to deal with in addition to half the population of Kiymako.

"What of your mother?" Ayuni asked.

"Betrayed also. Long ago."

Her expression softened. "You can't remember much either?"

"Not nearly enough. Sometimes, I think I can recall the words to a lullaby she used to hum. Among others, I have one memory of her tickling Snow when we were young, chasing him around the house."

Ayuni swallowed. "Did Father..."

A curse broke the din of conversation.

Two men seated in the corner of the room were arguing, a game of some sort arranged before them. "I have not cheated, not once," one said, hands raised. Rather than an expression of outrage, the young man appeared sad. Weary, even.

The other fellow swayed to his feet, flinging an arm out. "I was watching." He blinked, several times. His other hand was clenching and unclenching. "And I saw it, I'm sure it was you. You've got too many hands. I know it."

One of the men from the Temple stood, crossed the floor and hauled the fellow across to an empty seat at their own table. The angry gambler was muttering to himself but seemed inclined to sit. More, he now appeared a little unwell. Perhaps not unsurprising.

"I think now would be a fine time to seek our beds," Muka said.

Ayuni nodded.

Their rooms lay on the ground floor, set at the rear of the kitchen. Both were clean and well-appointed with bed, shelving, basin and mirror. The innkeeper apologised for only having two rooms, but Ayuni assured him it was fine.

"Thank you, My Lady. Please call upon me if you require anything," he said as he left.

"We can take this room if you wish, Ayuni," Never said. He moved to the window, opening the curtains to check on the lock. While there was no specific danger yet, there were still monks within the inn. The closer an eye he could keep on her the better.

Muka cleared his throat.

Ayuni blinked as she opened her mouth to speak, obviously at a loss for words. "This may sound odd, since I spent so much time alone in the temples, but that was not my choice, you see…"

"We understand," Muka said gently.

"Thank you, both. And you, Never. I know you want to watch over me," she said.

He cleared his throat. "Oh, well, that's what brothers do best."

Once she was gone he sat on the bed and began unlacing his boots, shaking his head as he worked. "I am a complete fool."

"No, you are right to worry," Muka said.

"I should have known she'd want some peace. Should have realised that even though we share blood, I am a stranger to her."

Muka put a hand on Never's shoulder. "Perhaps no stranger, Never. And do not fear, we sleep in shifts."

Never nodded.

Chapter 22

"Never, something has happened."

Never sat up, blinking at the morning light where it streamed through the open curtains. "What?"

Muka's silhouette resolved. His expression was one of concern but not fear. "Someone wishes to hire us."

Never ran his hands through his hair. "Really?" He found his water flask and drank, emptying it. "That's certainly a relief; I haven't had steady work for quite some time."

"It's an escort job for the Temple."

Never tapped a finger on the flask a moment, then grinned. "This is actually an opportunity, Muka."

"Never, I don't—"

"Trust me. Where better to hide but in plain sight? We already know Iri's charm works. Where are they travelling?"

He folded his arms. "East. To the forest."

Never chuckled. "Merciful Pacela, this is a true stroke of fortune. Why don't we hear them out?"

Muka muttered something beneath his breath but he eventually gave a short nod. "I'll bring Ayuni; they want to meet in the stable."

Never was already jamming his few belongings back into his pack. He splashed water over his face from the basin, then left the key with the innkeeper on his way out, speaking only a few words. But the fellow didn't even blink – the black fang held.

A misty cloud covered half the sky, rolling down from the north, but the stable was bright enough to see the muddy tracks from previously-departed travellers, along with Muka and Ayuni standing with a pair of temple men. They did not have the bearing of warrior-monks, despite the daggers at their belts. Instead, their soft voices and sun-burnt skin spoke of folk better accustomed to the indoors.

Horses were being readied beyond the pair; saddlebags and cinch straps checked by drivers and guards, these men more heavily armed with bows or tyrants. Others were tying down ropes on the loaded wagons, three in total.

"We're already two men short," one of the monks was saying. "And now that Daisoa has fallen ill too, we can't afford to be picky. They'll have to do."

"Greetings," Never said.

The second man scowled at Never. "About time."

Muka gestured to Never. "As I said, we two can easily make up for whatever shortcomings you feel my daughter presents to taking this task – one which you requested of us."

The oh-so-cheerful monk pointed at Muka. "Fine, but don't slow us down – and if we're set upon by bandits, you do your share, got it?"

"Of course – so long as when we reach Yalinamo you pay our share."

"Bah." The man stormed off.

The first monk offered a wheezing laugh. "Ah, please

forgive his temperament. He'll settle once we're on the road."
Then he joined his fellow at the lead wagon. The second
already had something of a formation beside it, which left
the role of rear guard. Only one other fellow had led his
mount beside it. The driver was leaning on his knees, whip
in hand.

"Ready for an adventure?" Never asked Ayuni and Muka.

Ayuni nodded, her eyes were alight. Perhaps it was the
thought of new experiences, new freedom, or the notion of
heading closer to her mother, but Muka only said, "Phoenix
watch over us."

They mounted up, Ayuni taking one of the pack horses,
and the line of wagons left the roadside and started east.

Never let his mount slow so he could watch Ayuni, who
was riding easily, her face uptilted to enjoy the sun. Muka
rode beside her, focused on the surrounding fields. Never
couldn't stop a flash of guilt – his own diligence was a little
lacking.

"Welcome, friend." The other guard spoke quietly.

It was the young gambler with the sad expression from
the night before. "Thank you," Never replied.

"It was kind of you to replace Daisoa."

"He seemed quite unwell; is he going to recover?" Never
asked. So far, the charm seemed to be holding up, despite
the relative distance from Muka and Ayuni. Perhaps his
accent was getting better or maybe the general surroundings
and the act of being hired, of other's acceptance, was enough.

"In time, I'm sure. I found him to be rather delicate for a
caravan guard."

"It didn't seem like his first job," Never said. He looked to
the wagon, where stacks of wooden boxes marked with the

Phoenix were arranged. "So what are we protecting?"

"The monks do not say." He met Never's gaze, and once more, Never was struck by the fellow's mournful expression. "Secrets weigh heavily upon a man, do they not?"

"Indeed," Never replied, unable to stop a slight frown. Was the fellow probing, did he suspect something was amiss?

Yet the guard's next words were to excuse himself. "I trust you won't take undue offence if I keep my own company for a time?"

"Please."

The fellow nodded then turned to gaze at the scenery, his bearing at ease and more, somehow exuding the sense that he was now actually alone. Never tapped his horse's flanks with his heels and joined Ayuni and Muka, sharing his experience.

Muka glanced over his shoulder. "Perhaps the charm was not wholly effective and he only sensed *something* unusual about you?"

"Perhaps he is a monk himself," Ayuni said. "I know many within the temple that are quite pensive."

"He bears watching in any event," Muka said.

Never nodded; he planned to do just that. And for the rest of the day he did, but the man did not slip to the head of the line to speak with the monks, nor did he speak again even when Muka or Ayuni rode near.

At night, each group of guards, including the driver, sat around their own fire – posting watch and eating quietly. Again, their morose friend added nothing, but the driver, a rangy man from the north named Esiang, was more jovial. In a cheerful voice he shared stories of time as a driver, including once when he swore he saw the Great Phoenix.

"Far to the north, near the mouth of the Soh River, a long time ago. I was a green lad, my first journey for a merchant. I knew my work when it came to the animals, but nothing had prepared me for the terrible cruelty of man. Our wagons had been attacked earlier, and though we drove the bandits away I saw so much blood that I thought I'd never sleep again. And so I was awake, staring up at the stars, when I saw it – a figure flying across the sky – like a person with wings!" His eyes were alight with the memory, as though he'd not forgotten a single detail. "I remember the statues mother had when I was young, too. It was a *woman* with wings of flame, and what I saw, it was just like that. But I think it was a man flying, though I can't be sure. I can find peace when I need to now, by thinking back to that night; and that's how I know the Great Phoenix is real."

Questions followed his tale but Never did not add his own; such troubling thoughts were best left unsaid. Based on Esiang's age, there was every chance such a mysterious shape had been Father. What was he doing in Kiymako, so long ago? Back then, it wouldn't have been a search for Ayuni's mother. Perhaps a different mate?

By the morning of their third day on the eastern highway – still three more to Yalinamo, the fields had given way to undulating grasslands dotted with hills and occasional stone relics. Once, during their noon meal, the wagons stopped near enough to one that Never sought permission from the ever-pleasant Garugi to examine one. The man complained but did eventually wave him off.

"Want to take a closer look then?" he asked Ayuni and Muka where they sat on a pair of bone-white logs.

Ayuni stood. "Yes."

Muka stretched his legs out, taking another bite from a large strawberry. "Why don't you two enjoy yourselves? I've seen them before."

A crumbling ridge of overgrown grass led up to a small hilltop where the ancient statue rested. Unlike the more common phoenix statues he'd seen in Kiymako, this was something else. Half-buried in earth, it was a large dome covered in small rectangular protrusions. Whoever had carved it had taken great care to make them regular in size too. Many had been worn down by wind and rain. Other pieces were broken and chipped but enough remained to give the impression of some long-forgotten creature sleeping in the earth.

Ayuni knelt, reaching out to touch the stone. The moment her fingers brushed the surface she jerked them back. "It's cold – like it's frozen."

Never joined her, reaching out with the back of his birch hand, and flinched at a sudden heat. "Like fire for me," he said. The Amouni came to mind – his usual suspicion, but there was little else to learn without a shovel. And even before Garugi, Never didn't care for blisters. He stood. "This might be something to investigate later; it does seem odd – whether it's Amouni or not."

"Our forefathers have been everywhere, haven't they?"

"They once ruled all the lands," he said with a nod. "Though the pattern doesn't strike me as Amouni, necessarily."

"Like your knife?" she asked.

He drew the Quisoan blade. "This one?"

"Yes. Is that what the triangles represent?"

He handed her the weapon. "No, this is from Mother's homeland – Quisoa. A young woman gave me this during the invasion."

Ayuni ran her fingers over the pattern a moment before holding it out but Never shook his head. "Why don't you keep it? You wear no blade. Think of it as a last line of defence."

"I'm not sure it would feel right to carry a weapon; I want to heal others."

He smiled. "Then think of it as a gift from your brother who doesn't want to worry."

Ayuni blinked back sudden tears, running her fingers again over the blade almost tenderly. "I... they didn't let me keep anything; nothing was really mine in the temple." She returned his smile. "Thank you."

"Let's return then," he said.

Ayuni joined him and they started back toward the wagons. A breeze picked up, tugging at her hair. She pushed it behind her ears, catching several stray strands. So far, Iri's colour had not worn off. "Never, can I ask you something?"

"Please."

"Why did you come to Kiymako now? I've been wondering, how did you learn of me?"

"Before he died, Snow told me that our father had been here, that he was sure you existed. Snow showed me a vision of Father painting the rune for protection on a Temple door."

Her eyes widened slightly. "He did that for me?"

"Yes. A touching gesture from the man who abandoned us both," Never said, unable to keep a sour note from his voice.

"Oh, Never. I didn't mean—"

He sighed. "I'm sorry. Forget about me, I'm still angry. Tell me, is Yalinamo a city of walkways suspended in the trees?"

"Yes. It's quite old. Apparently, its foundations were built by an older people."

"Then that is the temple I saw in my vision. Father left you there because he trusted the temple. Or perhaps because it was closer. I wonder."

"I cannot speak for our father, but I will say there are some I trust in the Divine Temple of Yalinamo, people who raised me until Brother Hiruso came to take me. After that, I was shipped off from temple to temple."

"And why did he come?"

"I cut myself in the garden while pruning a juniper tree. We were trying to save it. The next day, Sister Sikoka woke me, overjoyed. The tree was green again, returning with much vigour. Of course, she was duty bound to report what had happened to Mondami and after that, Brother Hiruso arrived and the tests began."

Never frowned. Sister Sikoka ought to have put her duty to Ayuni first. But he said only, "You are strong to have survived such a dark time."

"I had help then and I have you now. That makes it easier."

"Sister Sikoka?"

"And others. But she was the one to teach me everything mother didn't get the chance to share. She even told me about foreign lands and their wonders, like the ice tower in the Vadiya Mountains or the Silver City in Hanik. I know there's no way, but I wish I could see Sikoka again when we pass through."

"We might be able to send her a message, at least," Never said. He paused at a commotion from below – Garugi was motioning for them to hurry, as the wagons were lining up to leave.

Never raised a hand in acknowledgement. "I guess we better not keep him waiting, he's likely to lose both his arms if he keeps that up."

"I think you're right – maybe we should slow down," she said, a mischievous gleam in her eye.

Never laughed.

Chapter 23

The next morning, Never found himself riding through the pleasant sun with Muka and Ayuni alone – their quiet friend was gone. There was no sign of the guard on the plains, nor their back trail and so unassuming had the fellow been since leaving the inn, that Never hadn't even noticed his absence until mid-morning. "Let me ask," he said as he started toward the front of the line.

Yet his horse had barely taken half a dozen steps before the rumble of hooves reached him, a sound that was growing rapidly. A crossroads waited ahead, and thundering down from the north, was a long line of mounted warriors. As they neared, Never marked a red strip across their tunics.

Muka and Ayuni joined him. "Say as little as possible if we're questioned," Muka said. "Those are the Isansho's men from Mondami."

"Pressed into service for the Temple, it seems," Ayuni added.

Never reached up to pat the charm beneath his clothing. "Let's see how lucky this fang is." The line of warriors had already reached the head wagon and were waving for the monks to bring the train to a halt. "If they realise something is amiss, I'll try to lead them away."

"How?" Ayuni asked, concern in her voice.

He grinned, despite his own worry. "Let's save the surprise."

Now the warriors were heading down the line. They had a more unified look in hair, clothing and weapons, many with *sisan*'s and bows. Never frowned; wonderful, he might have to give them some target practice.

The soldiers were efficient in their search, swarming over the wagons and speaking a few words to each guard, each driver then moving on. Two men addressed Muka. "We are seeking two fugitives travelling with a young woman," the first said.

"One of the men is a foreigner, from Marlosi," the second added. His eyes were narrowed, as though he expected disobedience perhaps. "Have you seen anyone matching that description?"

"None. It's been a dull trip so far," Muka said easily.

He grunted. The first man didn't seem to be paying attention to Muka anymore, he was focusing on Ayuni and Never. A slight frown marred his features and he rubbed at a thin beard. Whenever his eyes moved from Ayuni to Never, he blinked several times.

Never fought the rising tension within him, lifting a knee to lean against the wagon.

"Look inside and let's go," the second man said as he left.

"Right," the first warrior replied, still sounding a little unsure. But he checked between the boxes beneath the covering then hurried after his superior without a backward glance, apparently having accepted that his doubts were unfounded.

Ayuni exhaled heavily. "I thought he was going to see through the charm."

"Another trial passed," Muka said, his faint smile a little wider this time.

"Onward, then," Never said.

Once the wagons had started forward once more, mostly to the tune of Esiang's grumbling about the delay from the driver's seat, Never leant back in his saddle and closed his eyes a moment. Nothing like a narrow escape to test the nerves. He let his mount lead, reins held only loosely as the day wore on.

"Never?"

He opened his eyes. Had he dozed? By the changed light, it was already afternoon. Ayuni rode beside him. "Yes?"

"What did you mean by surprise back there? I don't want you to do anything foolish for me."

He smiled. "Sorry, that's an older brother's job."

"I'm serious, Never." She gave him a stern look. "Just promise me you'll be careful."

A cry of alarm rang out from the van, cutting off his reply.

Men were leaping up from all around the line of wagons, covered in grass and brush. An arrow thudded into the side of the nearest wagon. Never swore, even as he wheeled his horse. If he'd been paying attention he might have noticed the ambush.

Muka obviously had, his sword was already drawn and he was charging to meet the four men who were attacking from the rear. Ayuni had pulled her mount closer to the wagon and was cupping her hands, a frown of determination on her face. Never kicked his horse forward, pulling two blades and throwing at one of the men trying to flank Muka.

The first dagger went wide by a narrow margin but the other grazed the man's upper arm. The minor wound caused the fellow to pause, and then Never's horse crashed into him with a whinny. Never fought for control, keeping his seat long enough to catch sight of Muka swinging his tyrant, slicing through limbs as he downed the remaining men.

A roar of flame followed.

Ayuni had raised her hand, flickering blue and green flame spearing across the road to engulf one of the attackers. At the next wagon, the other guards seemed to hold the upper hand with what appeared to be bandits, now that Never had a moment to truly see them. But further along, the lead wagon was under a more concentrated attack. Several guards were down with arrows and the two monks, Garugi and Fuda, were no-where to be seen.

"Muka?"

"On my way," he said, and charged to the lead wagon.

Never moved to Ayuni, who was breathing hard. The whites of her eyes were showing too. "I saw his face right before..."

"It's not easy, I know, but there will be time for that later," he said, keeping an eye on the struggle.

"It was different the first time... I was just running. Lashing out at anything that came too near."

He met her troubled gaze. "You did the right thing, Ayuni."

She nodded.

Never checked on the bodies he and Muka had dealt with, none so much as twitched, then back to the fighting.

Muka was already turning the tide, his movements precise and flowing – and he wasn't even using his *lunai*, he was simply a masterful swordsman. A shorn limb spurted blood, another man collapsed over Muka's sword, and a third met Muka's blade with his own, only to be struck down.

And then naught but the rasp of heavy breathing from the survivors followed.

Ayuni was tying her reins to the wagon. "I can help the wounded."

Never stepped before her. She had a kind heart but it could land her in trouble if she wasn't careful. "Ayuni..."

"Not with my blood," she said. "I've been taught a little herb-lore. Let's see what they have."

Together, they headed for the front, checking on the guards, most of who would need bandages at the least. One of the men who'd taken an arrow had already died, Ayuni's expression tightened when she saw him. But one of the drivers carried a heavy steel box and within, bandages and herbs and vials. Not enough for everyone but something. Ayuni thanked him and started organising the contents.

"I'll check on Muka," he said.

Ayuni nodded without looking up from her work. Never moved a little way further, to the lead wagon, where he found Muka standing before the two monks. Fuda was trembling but Garugi wore a dark scowl.

"How could they have known?" the man was demanding to no-one in particular. He seemed upset, certainly, and with cause, but Never again had to wonder exactly what was being transported.

"Perhaps it was planned for any who might pass," Muka suggested. He had sheathed his sword and seemed unharmed.

Garugi grunted. "It may be so."

"If I could interrupt?" Never asked.

"Why? Has anything been taken?"

"No. But someone has disappeared." Never described the sombre man. "He was working with us on the rear wagon and he's simply gone."

"Who?"

"I don't know his name. He was gambling with Daisoa in the inn."

Fuda shook his head. "I'm afraid I cannot place him."

Garugi folded his arms. "Nor I. But it is convenient that so soon as he flees, we are attacked. Check the bodies, perhaps he is among them."

Never nodded and Muka joined him, starting the unpleasant task. Yet of the thirteen men who had attacked – and died – none bore any resemblance to the missing guard. "He is more than he seems then," Muka decided after they'd reported to Garugi and started back.

"But what was his purpose here?"

"If it was to set the ambush in motion then return to share in the spoils, he would have seen what happened and left by now. Or began putting something else in place."

"For the cargo?" Never asked. "He did mention something about secrets."

"It's possible – the temple does transport valuables, silks, medicines and sometimes large quantities of gold or silver but I have to wonder if that is the case now."

"And yet he seemed so disinterested in everything else. He barely spoke after that first day..." Never rubbed at his neck. "Bah. I feel like I'm close to realising something."

"Well, we know we can probably blame him for having

been caught up in this," Muka said. "Or even thank him, if you think about it."

"Thank him?"

"I imagine our brush with the Isansho's forces earlier might not have gone so well had we not appeared to be a legitimate part of a Temple convoy."

Never slapped his thigh. "That's it! He did something to Daisoa, *that's* why he was too sick."

"Daisoa?"

"The man he was gambling with at the inn – and without who, we might not have been hired at all – you're right."

Muka nodded slowly. "If so, the stranger's purpose has grown murkier still."

"Could he be working for the Hammers?"

"I don't think we can afford to rule it out."

Never's gaze turned to Ayuni, who was smiling at one of the men as she wrapped a bandage around his wrist. "If so, we have to assume they'll soon know exactly where we are."

Chapter 24

It was a subdued camp that found itself seated around three cookfires. The night was too warm to need them for heat and they did provide light against the darkness and the possibility of another attack. Surrounding the survivors in turn were the wagons and their horses, with one man each set to watch from the driver's seats.

Despite his worry, Never didn't think there'd be another attack so soon. It didn't seem that the bandits were so strong; their clothing was especially worn and some of their arrows had obviously been repaired. More than a few bodies had been quite gaunt too.

Esiang wasn't convinced; the driver told no tales, simply sat and ate his rice. Conversations from the other fires were quiet too, as though everyone had one ear on the plain.

But an undercurrent of anger had risen from Garugi and Fuda's circle.

"I know what I saw," someone demanded, one of the bigger guards. "It was a flash of light, like unnatural fire. And it came from the new man's daughter. We all saw the burned body, what do you think caused it? I've been trying to tell you."

Ayuni looked up from her food, which she had hardly attacked with gusto.

"Be ready," Never said. How long had they been discussing it now? Must have been brewing since the immediate aftermath of the attack – he should have foreseen such a response. Some protector he was proving to be.

Muka already had one hand on the hilt of his tyrant.

Other conversations had stopped now. Garugi rose, leading his group over to Never's fire. The big guard pointed at Ayuni when he arrived. "I swear it, Brother Garugi, she made the fire – she's a sorceress."

"Maybe that's why we were attacked?" another voice suggested. "They're looking for her."

Echoes of agreement came from others.

Never and Muka stood as one. He motioned for Ayuni to do the same, stepping just in front of her to confront the monk and the accuser. "You know that doesn't make any sense. Poor bandits have no need for Ayuni; they were seeking whatever valuables we transport."

The guard started to answer but Garugi raised a hand. "Enough, Bao." He surveyed the camp. "Whatever this young woman is, it is clear she is a danger to us all. Who knows who she will bring down upon us next? And for all we know, you are accomplices with whoever tipped off the brigands. You must leave, each of you."

Never folded his arms. "I see. So, in order to better ensure the safe delivery of your cargo, you're going to reduce your numbers? Dazzling leadership, Brother Garugi."

The man's nostrils flared. "Fool! Leave or we will force

you."

Yet many of the faces turned away, lit orange by the fires. Of those who did not immediately jump to their feet, many bore bandages or other evidence of Ayuni's care. And maybe some were remembering just how effortlessly Muka dispatched his share of the thieves.

But neither did they rise to disagree with the monk.

"Please," Fuda said as he stepped forward. "It really is for the best. You may take your horses." He did not seem to be agreeing with Garugi, so much as acknowledging the fact that a fight would not end well for many.

"We accept," Ayuni said before Never could answer. "Thank you, Brother Fuda."

"Then be quick about it," Garugi said before returning to his fire.

Never glared after the man but Ayuni was right to prevent him from throwing out another quip. But oh, how he wanted to. Instead, Never joined Ayuni and Muka in collecting their belongings and unhitching their mounts. Never rubbed the neck of his mare as he did, glancing over his shoulder.

No-one followed them, nor did they watch.

"Let's find some shelter then," he said.

"At least we won't be rained on," Ayuni replied with a smile. She put a hand on his arm. "Forget them, Never."

He sighed. "I will. But if that's their idea of gratitude..."

"Let's not give them a chance to reconsider their foolishness," Muka said as he threw a leg over his saddle.

They crossed the grass and returned to the road at a walk, allowing for their eyes to adjust. The stars were a glittering army above but no moon yet – still, it was enough to travel by.

Time seemed to pass quickly from leaving and finding a suitable campsite on a small hill; the leeward side of one of the strange, broken stone domes. Travellers had dug out the space a little, revealing more patterned stone and creating enough room for a firepit and their three bedrolls.

"See?" Ayuni said. "In finding this place, we've been granted some good fortune already."

"Well, we deserve it," Never said with a chuckle. Her ability to maintain high-spirits was surprisingly welcome – so different from Snow. He had to wonder, was this what a normal sibling relationship was meant to be like? "And allow me to take first watch. I don't want any surprises."

"Do you think they will follow us?" Ayuni asked.

Never glanced at Muka. "No. But Muka and I have a theory about the guard who disappeared – he may have been working for the Hammers."

"Truly?" Ayuni frowned as she shook out her bedding. "Doesn't he seem like a strange choice for spy? Conveniently placed in that inn, too."

"We're not convinced ourselves," Muka said. "But we cannot dismiss him."

She nodded. "I'm happy to take my turn."

"I'll be up top," Never said.

He climbed around the hill to find a vantage point that allowed a fair view of the road then leant against the stone – only to flinch back... but there was no flash of fire. Had the first encounter with the strange stone been a sign or a warning? No way to know; it could have been any number of things. But it seemed this stone dome was no more than stone.

Perhaps there were no traces of Amouni cities or towns in Kiymako. Or maybe not here at least. After all, the thing lurking beneath the Sundered Road knew about Ascended Amouni. Which meant it was either incredibly old or it had encountered Father. And then there was Brother Hiruso too – he knew something.

Too much, no doubt.

Never checked on the now risen half-moon. How long had he been sitting against the stone? He stood and stretched his legs and arms, then adjusted his cloak so he could try his wings. Too long since he'd had a chance to check on them, how had they been healing? Slowly, he stretched them out – wincing at the tenderness, but he was able to extend them to their full span.

He brought his wings close around his body, then unfurled them a few times. All seemed well. If he needed, he'd be fine to fly.

A gasp hissed in the night.

Never spun, but it was only Ayuni. She was gaping at him where she stood, her face almost luminous beneath the moon.

"Never?"

"I take it Father didn't ever mention this?"

"Ah, no." She crept forward. "I can hardly believe... may I touch them?"

"Of course." He moved closer, then extended a wing. Ayuni ran her fingertips across his feathers, a gentle sensation, her eyes alight. "I have to keep them hidden for obvious reasons."

"Indeed." She looked up after a moment longer. "How is this possible? Even for Amouni?"

"I am Ascended." Never explained something of the

differences, sparing her some of the details of how he ascended. "Legends always speak of Amouni as rulers of the other peoples but seem to say little about their hubris."

"I remember Father telling me I was extra special to him, but not why. As a child it made it easier to deal with his absence. When I grew older I thought he meant my healing..." She frowned. "Wait. What hubris?"

"Ancient Amouni sought to control everything about those they had set themselves up to protect. For some, that meant slavery, as Amouni established themselves as governors and for others, such arrogance was taken right down to the dark depths of meddling with the qualities people possessed."

"What do you mean by that?"

"I once met a man that had been... changed, so that his body could pass through solid objects. He was once normal, but he was altered via ancient Amouni methods. I believe the Amouni of old could also control the kinds of strengths and weaknesses a person was born with."

"By the Phoenix," Ayuni breathed. "What happened to the man you met?"

"I do not know. He wanted to serve me as Master, but I sent him to live his own life. I hope it was not a mistake; he had been twisted by what had been done to him."

Ayuni hesitated. "Do you know who hurt him so?"

"Yes. It was Snow."

"Oh."

He smiled gently. "You should get some more rest, Ayuni. Muka will wake you when it's time."

She nodded and started back around the hillside, but paused. "Never?"

"Yes?"

"Do you think that Father had something like that in mind for me?"

"I think it's what he wanted for all his children."

"Then he was trying to rebuild the Amouni race, that was his own hubris, wasn't it?"

"Sadly."

Ayuni shifted her feet and did not speak for a long moment. She seemed to be fighting tears – and he could hardly blame her. "When he told me I was special..." She stamped a foot, even as she shook her head, seemingly at herself. "This shouldn't upset me so, I shouldn't be surprised."

Never did not answer; he didn't want to be the one to say aloud what she seemed to be realising on her own.

"It was because I was a woman. He expected me to bear Amouni children."

He crossed the distance between them and took his little sister into his arms.

Chapter 25

The forest of Yalinamo stretched before them on the horizon; a dark green line beneath the blue, distant yet, though Never expected to reach the trees before nightfall. If strange, disappearing guards or the Three Hammers didn't delay them. So far, the only people Never had passed on the eastern highway were travellers or merchants, most leading long wagon trains with extensions to carry piles of bamboo or other timber.

Ayuni had seemed more composed when they'd set out. He'd asked Muka to let her sleep through and now she was standing in her saddle, shading her eyes against the bright sun. "I think I see a road-side temple ahead. I'd like to visit it to pray."

"Is that safe?" Never asked.

"Such temples are tiny – two rooms only, for travellers. I don't think I've ever visited it... but if you think it's too dangerous, I understand."

He looked to Muka then back to Ayuni. "You two know the Temples better than I. What are the risks?"

"Communication between the temples is swift. At a stretch, it's possible a roadside shrine like this will have means to communicate with Mondami or Yalinamo," Muka said.

"You mean the opals?" Never asked.

"Yes. Though contrary to the rumours you may have heard, not every temple has them," he said.

"All the divine temples and city temples do," Ayuni said. "Many others also, but few road-side temples. They are too valuable to risk."

Never untied his charm and handed it to her. "Just to be safe."

"I will be swift," she said.

When they reached the shrine, which was as she'd described, small, with a low roof and a statue of the Phoenix at the entrance, Ayuni ducked within. Never kept his hood raised and positioned Muka between himself and the windows. Perhaps an ineffective precaution if he'd already been marked but why invite trouble if he hadn't? There was plenty of trouble around without him seeking it.

"What can we expect in Yalinamo?" Never asked Muka as he watched a tiny robin hop across the statue, pecking at insects as it did.

"It is similar to most Kiymako cities. The temples are a major force and the Isansho works with them more often as not. But Yalinamo folk are close to the forest and the *hin* that inhabit it."

Hin. The word was familiar, hadn't Hanael said it was like Marlosi for spirit? "How so?"

"Some people have contracts with the *hin* – in exchange for being fed, the *hin* will perform certain tasks for them.

The task might be finding a lost item, helping a garden grow or even cleaning and other duties of the house."

Never raised an eyebrow. "Cleaning? What are they being paid?"

"*Lunai.*"

"Isn't that dangerous?"

"They usually do not need much to perform their tasks – and without it, they wouldn't be able to in any event. The Temple believes the *hin* are actually manifestations of excess *lunai* to begin with, and that centuries of human attention and interaction have given the *hin* some manner of sentience."

"No-one has ever spoken of this to me before; I'm quite curious."

"I believe in Hanik and Vadiya, people call the *hin* by another name and think of them only as children's stories from 'that strange island' across the sea," Muka said. He frowned a moment. "Fairies, I think is the word they say."

"In Marlosa we have them too, and they are said to make the wheat ripen during harvest, but it is a tale for children."

"Well, the *hin* are real, and no doubt you will see them," Muka said.

Ayuni appeared in the doorway. She wore a serene expression now as she hurried across the road to return the fang. Did she truly feel better or was she hiding her pain? Doubtless she'd had to do so for most of her life. "The temple was empty."

"Is that something we need to worry about?" Never asked.

"No, not all road-side temples are attended each day."

"Someone from one of the villages probably visits," Muka added.

Never slipped the fang over his head and hid it beneath

his tunic before urging his horse forward once more. "Good. Let's cover a little ground then, I want to reach Yalinamo or anywhere with hot food and a proper bed."

The sun was starting its long dive when they finally reached the edge of the Yalinamo Forest. It reared up, a mighty wall of dark pine trees, needles still in the dying warmth of late afternoon. The road drove in straight and true, eventually lost in shadows at the limits of Never's view.

And flanking the entry were two mighty trunks, their tops missing, standing like giant pillars. Even so, they still rose half a dozen storeys high and would have measured nearly as wide as a house.

"The Red Gates," Muka said. "Said to have been cut and set in place by the Green God to welcome us to his abode. In myth, there were once arches of golden thread spun between them and any who climbed to the top was rewarded with an audience with him, where he would, if you were found worthy, grant you a single boon."

"Had anyone climbed it?" Never asked.

"It is said that none could do so, for earthly hands were too coarse, earthly bodies too heavy. The arches broke one by one under the stubbornness of humanity until they were all gone and then no-one could try ever again."

"Ah. Sad but unsurprising, I think."

"Within, the highway will eventually turn north to Yalinamo. We have four, five days before we reach it."

"And how many opportunities to be ambushed again?"

"Many. If the Hammers truly do know where we are then this will be a dangerous next few days," Muka said.

"It might be a chance to lay a trap of our own," Never said.

"Any ideas?" Muka asked as they rode between the trunks.

"Not yet but give me time."

The air beneath the trees was cooler, the shade welcome, though patches of light were still plentiful as the trees did not clump together until further in. Now, on the edges of the forest, there were plenty of gaps between the large pines, fewer saplings and a heavy covering of old needles on the ground, smothering undergrowth.

The swift warbling of robins filled the branches as they rode.

"Peaceful," Never said after a time.

Occasionally they passed branching trails, some faint, some well-used. Ayuni knew what lay at the end of each, be it village, ruin, or bamboo farm. "I used to see them through the bars of my window," she said. "Once they told me which path led where, I would memorise them to make the trip seem faster."

Before full dark they found a well-concealed campsite between the trees. The forest had grown steadily thicker as they travelled, enough that there was no clear line of sight from their camp and the highway.

All of which suited Never fine as he sifted through the greying ashes of an old campfire. A melted piece of steel caught in the shape of a horseshoe lay within, perhaps it had been a necklace once. He tossed it into the pine needles and started arranging twigs and smaller branches for their own fire.

"Tomorrow we can take a bed at the Blueberry Inn," Muka said. "I know the owner, she will treat us well."

"Will we place her in danger by staying there?" Ayuni asked. "I've not heard the Hammers to be careless, but I would still worry."

"She is a strong woman, but I will warn her. Like you, I have only ever heard of the Hammers as being creatures of dread precision."

Ayuni drew forth a pot and skillet – part of the goods they'd been afforded by the generosity of Fuda – and handed them to Never. "Get the pan hot; I think we have some eggs here."

"Yes, ma'am."

She waved a carrot at him, fixing Muka with a look too. "And this time you better let me do my share. I'll take the first watch, no arguments."

Never raised his hands and Muka offered his faint smile.

Chapter 26

The village of Tisura appeared nearer to the image in Never's vision of his father, with half the homes resting aground, and the other half suspended in the trees and connected via bamboo walkways with hand rails. Coloured ribbon had been tied to the walkways, hanging before the buildings, bright beneath the morning light. The colours were grouped together and seemed to mark different parts of the village; even the Blueberry Inn – which rested on the ground below – bore a flag of dark blue over its entry.

A few villagers greeted them as they approached the inn, many of whom were heading into the woods with axes and saws. Muka led them to the inn's stable, where he paid the stable hand to care for their horses, then he took them into the common room, where a softly spoken monk sat before a group of children, who were in turn, seated on the floor.

"And after that night, said to be the longest night, the Phoenix was reborn and rose from the scorched land and the great bird of fire took to the skies then, and flames dripped from each wing, falling down upon the people."

A little boy gasped.

The monk smiled. "Worry not, Haon. For the people did not burn – do you know what happened?"

He shook his head, but two other children raised hands. "I know, Brother Wikaru, please?"

"Very well."

"The sparks went into everyone's heart." One young lad beamed.

"Exactly," Brother Wikaru said. "And those sparks became the kindness and caring that we all have within us."

"Even old Piromon?" another child asked.

"Yes. And it's up to us to keep the spark alive by caring for those around us, our family and friends, and fellow villagers."

A fine sentiment, but not one that would survive childhood. Never couldn't prevent a twinge of sadness at the sight of their earnest little faces.

The door creaked open and a greying woman approached Brother Wikaru.

He met her gaze and smiled. "Greetings, Fuo. Do you seek me to share your gratitude?"

"Yes, Brother."

"I will be but a moment longer."

"I'll find Teyeon," Muka said softly, heading toward a door that presumably led to the kitchen. As he did, Ayuni took a chair to listen to the monk but Never drifted to one of the windows, at the sound of a commotion in the street.

Two men were arguing over a broken crate. Melons littered the street; it seemed one man had walked into the other without realising. The argument began to ease somewhat, though the two men still had not reached an agreement, it was the fellow standing just beyond them that caught Never's eye.

The disappearing guard.

The same sombre expression rested on his face but now the young man wore clothing more suited to a monk; and bore no weapons. He gave Never a small nod, then moved on from the argument, slipping between two houses and heading into the trees.

"I'll be back soon," Never told Ayuni and dashed for the door.

He ran across the street, avoiding the arguing pair as he followed the mysterious man's trail. The houses flashed by, the rasp of a saw and scent of fresh pine fleeting as he stumbled onto a dirt crossroad. One path led up behind the row of homes and the other into the trees.

Brother Morose stood at some ways along the trail, resting against a trunk.

"Hey!" Never started forward and the man turned into the forest. Never quickened his pace, scratching his hand in his haste, before sliding to a halt before the tree. If the fellow was working with the Hammers, this was a fine way to lead Never away from Muka and Ayuni. Never drew a blade and resumed his pursuit, a little slower now, with one ear on his surroundings.

But there were no sounds beyond his own footfalls, no birds – and even the village seemed to have fallen under a cloak of silence as clouds covered the sun.

The faintest suggestion of a trail led Never deeper into the wood – and still no sign of the blasted man. Here, fallen branches were strewn across the forest floor and shrubs were pushing through the covering of needles. He climbed onto a grey log, then dropped into a crouch.

A pile of clothing sat before Never, a monk's dark green robe against the brown needles.

Yet the forest was empty.

Never crept forward. A small clearing lay ahead; he pushed between a sloping pair of trunks and found clear ground before an altar. It was no more than a square construction of large logs, now turning to rot but on its top stood a figure of carven stone.

The statue was that of a woman with a lovely smile, her face upturned to the sky, expression of peace so vivid that Never had to admire the sculptor. But it wasn't her face that captivated him, it was her wings. They spread behind her, in a glorious span that seemed as though they were wings of fire not feather.

As he stared, a flicker of movement appeared at the edge of his vision – a green butterfly with two yellow spots. It flitted closer, alighting on his hand, grazing the blood from his scratch. And then it flew away, disappearing into the trees.

He frowned.

Why had the phantom man led him here?

Never turned a slow circle but there was no doubt, he was the only one in the clearing.

***

"He disappeared, completely," Never explained where he sat with Ayuni and Muka in his room. He gestured to the robe. "That's all he left behind; I found it near the altar."

"The Phoenix as a woman," Muka said. "An unpopular belief among those placed high in the Temple now. In my childhood, it was much more common to see the Phoenix carved so."

"I would love to visit it, if we get the chance," Ayuni said, her eyes alight with curiosity.

Muka moved to the window, parting the curtains enough to see into the street. "As we leave perhaps. Which I am now unsure of when that should be."

"Our ghostly friend doesn't seem to have anything to do with the Hammers," Never said.

"It seems less likely now."

"We had planned to resupply here and continue on – can we reach the next village before nightfall?" Never asked.

"If we eat swiftly."

"That's still probably the best choice, isn't it?"

"I had wanted to use the inn as a haven to gather information. I hate being blind to the Hammer's movements," he said.

"The Temple might know," Ayuni said. "I'm sure either of us could pass as monks if needed."

"Such a thought had crossed my mind," he replied.

"Would a smaller village like Tisura have such informed monks?" Never asked. "Even with the opals? I can't imagine Hiruso contacting the temple here to let them know where he's sent the Hammers."

"True, but the opals are less a direct communication and more of a shared... pool of knowledge," Muka said. "Monks can draw from whatever is shared by the Grand Temple in Mondami."

"I see." Never grinned. "Then it looks like we're heading to worship, doesn't it?"

"I'm not sure Iri's charm is *that* strong, Never," Muka said.

"Hmmm. The temple would certainly be an unpleasant place to discover the fang's limitations."

Ayuni nodded. "It would be safer for you here."

"Probably," Never said. The very same thought echoed in his head but he did not express it aloud; he had to trust her. "But if you expect me to simply sit and be, then you're fools. I'll handle the supplies."

"Start with Teyeon," Muka said. "She'll know the best merchants."

"Right. Watch over each other," he said as they started toward the door. He followed them into the hall and to the now empty common room where he had to unclench his jaw and force his feet to stay put.

Stay, idiot.

The inclination to keep Ayuni in sight was the very thing that would put her in danger if he let it.

"Well then, can I feed you?"

Never turned to the bar. A tall woman leant on the wood, smiling. Her hair was shaven high like most women he'd seen, tied up in something of a topknot. However, her tunic revealed her upper arms, which bore their share of old scars.

"Teyeon?"

"I am. And you're Muka's friend? You're worried about the girl."

"My sister."

"Well, don't be. Muka won't let anything happen to her. Sit."

Never did as she offered. "I trust him but it's hard not to be the older brother."

"Well, let him take that role for now."

"Did I mention where they're going?"

"I heard you speaking before," Teyeon said, her expression still one of confidence. "Here, take a drink of this." She knelt, and the sound of bottles clinking followed. When she rose, she held a bottle of clear liquid that slid within the glass, almost slow, as though it were thicker than most alcohols.

She poured a small cup for him. "A moment longer."

Teyeon then produced a small circular tin. Pale powder rested within and she sprinkled it into the drink, stirring it with a spoon. A vivid blue swirled, chasing the spoon as she worked.

"This will help."

He lifted it and inhaled. A sour scent. "By keeping me wide awake? This is *batena* in here, isn't it?"

"Right. And the clear liquid is sometimes called Smiling Fool."

Never had to laugh; for he sensed no guile from her. "So what are you trying to do to me?"

"Take your mind off your worries."

"Let's see how that goes then," he said as he lifted the cup. The first taste was sharp and sour, and the texture bordered on unpleasant. But he took a bigger drink and found himself smiling by the time he set the cup back down. "I see what you mean."

Teyeon laughed. "There you go."

She told him several stories about her time as a warrior, how it helped when it came to dealing with drunks as an innkeeper, and once, a particularly persistent admirer. It seemed she'd known Muka a long time, they'd trained together but both left the Temple due to changes brought about by Brother Hiruso, not in the least, supplanting Wanatek with Isansho Shika.

"So she was chosen because she was willing to go along with whatever Hiruso is up to?" Never asked.

"Yes. Muka and Wanatek suspected that he was moving to supplant the Divine Throne. They could never prove anything. They at least wanted to be in a position to respond to any hostile moves."

He lowered his voice a moment. "Is it safe to talk so? I wouldn't want to bring unwanted attention down on your inn."

"Not to worry, all who work here are friend to Muka and I."

Never took another drink. "I've meant to ask him, but how did he earn the name Sword of Stone?"

"Ah, that is a simple tale. Do you know what the *tobake* is?"

He shook his head.

"It is a formal challenge, a test of a monk's *lunai*, I suppose – issued over grievances between warriors, and though I know the story I know not the reason behind it for he will not say."

"Sounds serious."

"I believe so. But the *tobake* pitted Muka against a dozen men – one after the other. He had to prevent each man from moving him, blade against blade. Of course, his challenger faced Muka last, hoping his *lunai* would have weakened." She paused to smile. "It had not. And since all failed, that is how he became known as Sword of Stone."

"I see you're hard at work gathering our supplies, Never." Muka stood in the doorway, Ayuni beside him.

Never raised his cup. It hadn't impaired his vision yet – or his judgement, but it was certainly a strong drink. "Teyeon forced me to drink with her."

"That I believe," he said as he approached the bar.

They took seats and Teyeon organised more cups – wine for Muka and the tart juice favoured by the Kiymako for Ayuni. "Bad news?" she asked them.

Muka nodded. "Yes. But we might be able to turn it to our advantage if Never's willing to take a risk."

He raised an eyebrow. "You say that like there's a chance I *won't* be willing to take a risk."

Chapter 27

"The Hammers were sent to Yalinamo but will not make it known to the temples when they have arrived," Muka explained.

"So that's the bad news?" Never asked. "That Hiruso has sent his hounds exactly where he expected we would be travelling? Not good news, precisely, but perhaps not a surprise either."

"That's part of it," Ayuni said. "But the orders are that I must be spared no matter the cost – even if it puts innocents in danger. Or kills them. Brother Hiruso wants you too, though not as much from what we learnt."

Never frowned.

"It gets more troublesome," Muka said. "There have been highly-accurate drawings of each of us shared between the temples and an impressive reward offered for anyone who helps apprehend us. If the population is also searching, we're significantly out numbered."

"And these drawings pre-date our disguise at least?"

"Yes," Muka said. "But that's where I think we need to

counter Hiruso's efforts by laying a false trail."

"Sounds good. What do you have in mind?"

"Let's show them the real Never a few times. Once in Sigawa at dawn, then in Akurik around noon and finally Okana before evening. Force people to chase rumours to make our path to the mountains easier."

Never was nodding slowly. "And these places you mention are far apart?"

"Yes, but perhaps not for someone with your gifts," Muka said.

"Then I'd better get some rest before dark – sounds like I'll be sharing the night with naught but the moon."

"I'll prepare a map," Muka said. "Even in the dark, Sigawa will be easy to find, and in order to beat the dawn you'll have to leave before midnight."

"Ah. My joy knows no bounds, hearing that." Curiosity glittered in Teyeon's eyes, but she did not ask what was doubtless on her mind and Never wasn't going to volunteer the information. He'd leave that up to Muka; best if the man decided whether Teyeon knowing more would endanger her any further. "Forgive me, we still need supplies."

"It's no trouble," Muka said.

"I'll bring you something to eat, if you like?" Ayuni asked.

"If I'm awake, that would be wonderful," he said as he started toward the room he shared with Muka. He blinked rapidly as he walked; maybe the Smiling Fool had been stronger than he realised – that or the *batena* had obviously not been very potent.

Once he had found his room, closed the door and curtains, removed his boots, most of his knives and his tunic and made himself comfortable, Never closed his eyes and drew in a series of long, deep breaths. He lay there in the growing dark, breathing and keeping still, but true sleep eluded him... he simply drifted in and out of full consciousness until a knock came at the door.

"Never?"

Ayuni with food.

Perhaps not a bad idea. "I'm awake," he called.

The handle squeaked as light bled into the room, Ayuni's silhouette following. The scent of spice reached him before she did and he rose to open the small lamp. Ayuni handed him his tray and sat on Muka's bed, but did not speak at first.

He lifted a fork and speared a piece of meat, eating a few pieces. Gamey, but hot and welcome. "You planning on watching me eat all of this?" Never asked with a smile.

Ayuni shook her head, and though she attempted a smile it seemed to break apart before it formed. "Never... I want to ask you something."

"Of course." He set his meal aside.

"I know we have not known each other long... but I feel safe with you, ever-since you found me." She tucked a lock of hair back behind her ear. "And so I feel like I have to ask before tomorrow because we're heading into such danger – you in Sigawa for a start and Muka and I in the road. The Hammers could be anywhere and there's the Temple too..." she trailed off, taking a shuddering breath.

"Whatever you ask," Never said. "You know I will do."

She nodded. "Thank you. Before I ask, however... will you tell me everything you have held back about our father?"

Never sighed. It wasn't fair to deny her the truth about her heritage – after all, he'd spent years searching for his own. He knew what it was to wonder and to have no answers.

And it would have been worse for Ayuni, since she'd spent years a prisoner, unable even to take her own steps. "I'm not saying I *won't* tell you all I know; but I fear you won't enjoy it."

"I am ready." Not a trace of hesitation in her voice.

"Very well." Never outlined all he knew, from what few memories of his own he still possessed – including the rape of his mother – to those given by Snow's vision, like the strange wolf-like creature. He reiterated the guesswork about the man's quest to sire more Amouni everywhere he went, and the stories created about Father throughout many lands.

"Then we may have many more siblings?" Ayuni asked. Her face appeared near-drained of colour, as it had been since hearing of the rape. But she hadn't asked him to stop, either.

Never shrugged. "I am not certain. One thing makes me unsure – why would Father's blood grant me a vision of Kiymako yet no-where else?"

"Then we are the last?"

"Perhaps of his line," Never said, before explaining about Cog.

"I see." Ayuni frowned. "But surely there are no other Ascended Amouni?"

"I do not believe so. Why?" He leant forward. "I know I have promised to tell you everything, but I do not know if I have the knowledge to unlock your wings – Snow may have taken that with him to the grave."

Now she did smile. "Do not fear; that is not my wish."

"Ah – you're concerned there could be more like our father."

"Yes."

"Snow told me that when Father was put to death by the old Empress of Marlosa they scattered his bones, and what remained I have locked away in Pacela's Temple," Never said. "None will come anew from Father – so as I said before, I fear he left only you and I. Unless you have any siblings by your mother?"

"No," she said. "There was only Mother and me."

"Was she a healer like you?" Never asked. "You have not spoken of her much."

"I know. Sometimes it's hard to remember without the pain of our separation added to the memories, even the happy ones. But she was a monk. Her role within the temple was unique I think, to our village. It was her responsibility to chronicle the lives of all who lived there – she used to teach me my letters by lamplight. I can still see her hands before me, quill moving steadily."

"She must have been not without influence then," Never said.

"I think at times." She smiled then. "One thing I do remember was a particular young man begging mother not to reveal the truth of his various indiscretions."

"I wonder if she ever wrote about our father."

"Not that she ever mentioned but no doubt I was too young. We will ask when we see her – I would love to read any such writings also," Ayuni said, then fell silent.

"So, what of your request?" Never asked.

"I have been thinking on what you told me, about Brother Hiruso. He inferred he knew Father."

"Yes. He seemed disappointed that Father had not taught me more about being Amouni."

"Then it is not beyond the realm of possibility that they knew one another, even that they shared a common goal – if that is true, Hiruso may have been keeping me for more than my healing abilities."

Never frowned – a rush of anger coming with it, though he kept his voice calm somehow. "Have you ever sensed he wishes for you to bear a child?"

"No, but perhaps he even *fears* the risks of childbirth? After all, if I were to die the healing salves they make will cease forever."

"Perhaps a valid fear. If we compare the amount of women Father attacked with his children and it would seem birthrates for Amouni are quite low."

"Exactly," she said with a grim nod. "But I wouldn't be surprised if Hiruso decided to take that risk if he was desperate enough to create *more* of my blood via a child. And if that happens, Never... I want you to promise that you will do everything you can to kill me before any birth occurs."

Never felt his eyes widen.

"I am serious. Considering my bloodline, he will no doubt place himself as father of any offspring, and such a child will be too terrible to contemplate."

"Ayuni..." Never moved to sit beside her. She had a point about the potential power of a child born of Temple and Amouni heritage but what she was asking was pure madness. He could not take the life of a sibling all over again. She was the last of his family; it was simply not possible. "I cannot. And you cannot know that is what he seeks."

"But I fear it, and who else can I trust? If we are captured tomorrow..."

Never took her hand. "If that happens I will find you."

"But what if you're too late? He may be desperate enough to risk a child now that you are here."

"If that was his plan he has waited years longer than he might have, Ayuni."

"I know. But it's still the most likely scenario, isn't it?"

"I will not let that come to pass," he said. "And neither would you – I saw what happened to the warriors who chased you."

"What if he can withstand even that?"

"He cannot. You are strong, Ayuni," Never said firmly. He tried to put all the confidence he had in her into the words, but he did not know if it was enough. "Don't forget that."

Yet she gave his hand a squeeze then stood. "Thank you. I should let you rest. Fly true, Brother."

"And you, Sister."

Chapter 28

Evening light cut through the pine and bamboo to fall onto the thatched rooves of Okana. For the third time that day, he found himself perched on a tree, staring down at those unaware – for now – of his presence.

That would change soon enough.

He'd left Iri's fang with Ayuni and Muka where it would do more good. Not that either of the two were defenceless if attacked; he had to remind himself of the fact as he'd flown through the dark sky, searching for the night glow of Sigawa where it winked on the horizon of the forest.

At dawn, he'd launched himself into a swooping dive, bursting through a market square, where early-risers waited for stall keepers to finish setting out their wares. Shocked cries followed him, and he made certain to bank in the air, to give more time to be seen. In the next town, Akurik, he pulled a similar stunt – tearing across a large clearing where a group of men and women were competing over coloured rings hurled through the air. Both teams – Never assumed that was their purpose – halted their movements to stare and point. Shouts rose up too – someone calling for a weapon it seemed, but he was already twisting up between the branches to disappear.

Now, perhaps a far grander gesture was warranted.

Word would have been spreading between the temples by now, and no one town or city would know where he'd appear next – but his previous acts had only been the appetiser. Now would come the main meal.

Okana had more homes amongst the trees, more walkways spanning them, but below there were shadowy paths and little movement. Perhaps a fitting place for a fountain of crimson-fire? It had to be deserted enough that he hurt no-one, but people had to see him too. The red light would draw attention...

Never leant out over the branch. Down below, a pair of men headed toward the outskirts of town. It was difficult to tell but one of the men seemed slender, his sharp features familiar, even from a distance.

Wanatek?

If it was the rebel leader, what was he seeking here in Okana? Anything Never attempted now would only draw unwanted attention down on the rebel, either directly or via any subsequent searches. The risk was too great; Never had to speak with Wanatek.

He hid his wings and started climbing down, muttering a curse when his hand burst a bubble of sap. At the sound of a hushed conversation below he paused, breathing a prayer to the surrounding pine needles – if any fell...

But the voices moved on. Never waited a moment before climbing a little further, then dropped softly to the ground. He circled the remaining houses on the edge of Okana and joined the trail Wanatek had used. He did not have to travel far to come across another home – this one set in a depression beneath the trees.

Light flickered within. Had the two entered? Who did they visit?

Or had they already moved on? In the near-dark it wouldn't be easy to track them, but he heard no small sounds of nearby travel. Never crept toward the house, approaching a window at a crouch. Behind the glass, warm light set a granite statuette of the Phoenix to glittering and voices drifted through.

"Are you sure about this? I cannot overstate the risk." Wanatek's voice.

"We do not wish to pressure you." This from a familiar-sounding voice – most likely Etsu, the short woman who'd led Never to his tent back in the Southern Reeds.

"I am sure. You know I have my own reasons to go along with yours." The third speaker was a younger woman.

"Very well. There is much we must prepare now, but thank you," Wanatek said.

Never waited as the sound of chairs moving followed. What were they recruiting her for? Obviously the rebellion in Najin, but what exactly was she going to do? Assassinate the Isansho?

He slipped away from the window.

Whatever they had planned, Never didn't want to bring it into jeopardy by causing a stir now. He could still light up the evening with some crimson fire, but perhaps in a smaller town between Okana and Yalinamo.

He circled away, putting some distance between himself and Wanatek before selecting a tree to climb, reaching for the lowest limb.

The faint swish of cloth against cloth came from behind.

Never rolled to the side. Something struck the ground where he'd stood. He came to his feet, knives in hand. A dark figure was reaching for whatever it had thrown – what looked like a net with weighted ends.

A breath alerted him to a second attack right before something hit him from behind – another net; the weights clunked into his hip and the heavy mesh bore him to the needle-covered earth. Never twisted, sawing at the netting but it was woven steel thread.

"Rest easy," a voice smirked from above.

Something wet splashed across Never's face, a cloying scent following. It was so strong that he gagged. The liquid stung his eyes – but the discomfort did not last, as true darkness smothered him, turning the net to gossamer.

***

A rhythmic pain drew him up from the depths of his drug-induced sleep, yet it was not enough to register full consciousness – the sun was bright, and a muted clacking sound lingered, but he could not stay awake.

***

When Never next woke it was to the sound of humming – a man's voice, an unfamiliar melody. Never opened his eyes, squinting against a strange light. He couldn't move his arms or legs; he was bound to a bed in a spacious room. He blinked. So spacious, that it bore a round pool set in the floor, immaculate marble edges encircling clear water.

Above, soft, blue-tinted light fell from a massive skylight; not unlike what he'd seen in the Amber Isle. The humming came from a silver-haired figure in the water; the man facing away from Never. Muscled arms spread across the pool, a giveaway probably as clear as the hair; it was hardly likely that a stranger had taken Never from Okana – it seemed Brother Hiruso had a flair for the dramatic too.

Or perhaps it was a character flaw.

"What did your thugs give me?" Never asked. His mouth tasted of ash.

The humming stopped. "Enough to ensure your cooperation, nothing more."

"How solicitous of you."

"Of course – you are quite valuable, even if your blood is not so potent as Ayuni's."

"Where is she?" Never demanded.

Hiruso turned, revealing a raised eyebrow. "No concern for yourself then?"

Now Never smiled, but it was a cold smile and he leant forward as far as he could manage, a bare gesture only. "You've already told me I am useful, so you clearly do not plan to kill me, which is more than I can say for my intentions toward you."

"Such spirit. Or stubbornness, perhaps." The monk swam across to where a towel waited, then rose, water streaming from his body – that of a seemingly much younger man – and wrapped himself in it before approaching the bed. Even his face appeared younger than before. At the bed, he took a stool and gestured to Never. "Yet your circumstances are hardly conducive to grand revenge."

"You don't hold every surprise."

"Don't I?" he chuckled. "You are of course, bluffing."

"Only until I'm not," Never said, yet it was bravado and no more. He had no weapons, no way to free his blood and more, he was bound and at a distinct disadvantage before Brother Hiruso's *lunai*, his strange defiance before the ravages of age.

"Well, in the meantime, let's share some information, shall we?"

"I see. Now we get to pretend we're just having a mutually beneficial chat."

Hiruso's brows drew together in a deep frown. "I am not pretending when I say you are not as useful as you perhaps think."

"Then why not just kill me, old boy."

"You cannot goad me into unleashing your blood, surely you know that."

"Because you are afraid."

Hiruso laughed.

Never only grinned at the monk. "You are afraid – you're afraid to die. Why else would you use Ayuni's blood to recapture youth and extend your lifespan."

Brother Hiruso's laugh took on a strained note for just a moment – so swift Never might have missed it had he not been waiting for it – but the man did not stop, did not lash out and nor did he acknowledge Never's barb, despite the way it had struck something of a chord. "Is that the limit of your vision?"

"It would seem so – but spare me your fanciful plans in any event. What do you think I can tell you?"

"Can you not guess?"

He could indeed. "You seek another sibling."

"Yes," Hiruso hissed. "If any exist as your father insinuated."

"And your offer?" Never kept his voice free of doubt; not too difficult considering his anger. Yet was Hiruso's passion born of certainty or hope? Father had not left behind other children. Never's own surety, that which he'd shared with Ayuni only yesterday, teetered momentarily.

"The truth about your father's time here in Kiymako," Hiruso said as he stood. "Allow me to give you the peace to think upon what you might gain simply by co-operating a little now."

The man walked across the room and to a door set in a deep recess, leaving without another word.

Never ground his teeth.

Bastard.

Somehow, it had all gone wrong in Okana. Had it been the Hammers who'd caught him? There had been at least two of them and they'd been well-prepared. What didn't make sense was how they'd known to be waiting in Okana at all. Had it been as Wanatek suggested? That Brother Hiruso was able to sense Never nearing?

Perhaps, it fit neatly enough with the man happening to be in the south-eastern village in time for Never's landing on Kiymako.

And if so, it seemed the monk could have pounced at any time during his travels. Why hold back? The obvious answer was that Hiruso had been waiting for Never to separate himself from Muka and Ayuni. So the monk *did* consider them a threat, after all, he'd arranged for the Hammers and had not appeared to challenge Never, Ayuni and Muka together.

More, the collection, drugging and transportation was another action that spoke to the lie in the man's words when he claimed Never was not so important.

Hiruso wanted more than knowledge of any surviving siblings.

The surface of the clear pool had long-since grown still when the skylight began to darken. Never had not come up with any other motives. At least, no reasons other than blood. Perhaps once he caught the muffled echo of footfalls beyond the nearest wall but nothing else until full dark, when a woman in a temple robe approached, her hood pushed back to reveal greying hair. She was thin – even bony – but she approached with a warm smile that banished the hint of austerity, holding a steaming bowl on a tray.

Never's stomach rumbled.

"Sounds like your stomach has been eating of itself in the absence of sustenance," she said.

"Lamentably."

"Let me," she said, taking Hiruso's stool. She set the tray across her knees and lifted a spoonful of stew, meat and peppers visible in a rich brown gravy. "I had it prepared as befitting an outsider. I hope it is suitable?"

Without any choice, Never opened his mouth and took a bite. It was good, as good as anything he'd had back home. "Thank you, Sister."

"It is a glad duty." She met his eyes, giving him a look of some... urgency? Then she spooned some sauce onto the tray and began writing with the spoon. Already the letters were running together – but the word was clear enough. *Friend.* Written in Marlosi.

Never looked up. The sister was lifting another spoonful to his mouth, which he ate.

"I am Sister Sikoka. Brother Hiruso has asked that I attend to you while you have been given time to reflect."

He chewed the mouthful but did not taste the food this time. Sikoka? The sister who'd looked after Ayuni! "I hate to burden you this way – since I am actually highly skilled at operating eating utensils and have been for some years, something I'd be most happy to demonstrate for you." He kept his tone light, but his eyes posed a question.

"I suspect that decision is above my role," Sister Sikoka said. She spilled more stew and wrote two words now: *Tomorrow* then *Night*.

"I suspected as much."

"Well, you're not my only responsibility, so let's keep eating before it gets cold," she said.

He nodded and continued the slow process of being fed. Once the stew was nearly done, Sikoka took the last of the gravy and wrote a final word – Ayuni, then smiled when she did so.

A bit of tension seeped from his body, replaced by a warmth that probably had as much to do with his relief as the hot food in his stomach.

Sister Sikoka offered another, smaller smile as she left.

Never let his head fall back against his pillow – perhaps a small mercy that he even had one – and prepared for a long wait. Sister Sikoka seemed trustworthy even if Never couldn't shake the memory of his conversation with Ayuni. Hard to ignore the feeling that Sikoka ought to have done more to protect Ayuni in the past... but maybe the older woman was going to atone now.

It was clear that the monk knew she was taking a serious risk.

And clear also that Hiruso had some way of listening in on whatever was said in Never's sparse prison.

But if Pacela was handing out merciful acts then she had exceeded herself this night if Ayuni, and presumably Muka too, were truly safe.

"I hope I'm next, Sweet Lady."

Chapter 29

Someone in the temple had affixed wheels to a chair, much like the arrangement the Bleak Man had, allowing Never to be tied in place and then pushed throughout the stone halls of Yalinamo Divine Temple – by Brother Hiruso himself.

The man seemed content simply to act as Never's chaperone, as he nodded to the occasional Brother or Sister, who passed quietly in their green robes, some carrying water while others, baskets of produce.

The interior of the place was mostly stone but potted plants of baby pine, fir, and bamboo lined the corridors. Some pots were huge; tall enough to reach Never's chest had he been standing and from them grew flowers arranged in pleasing splashes of pinks, blues and yellows. It brightened the temple – a floral facade for dark motives.

Tall windows let ample light into the building. Within each window alcove stood a bird carved in stone, wings spread as if about to thrust up from the earth. Each one bore a slightly different pose, so that, had he been sprinting by and watching the windows, the bird might have appeared to have been raising its wings.

"To symbolise that any rebirth is gradual," Brother Hiruso explained, doubtless having noted the direction of Never's gaze.

Never grunted.

"Let me show you something that will perhaps lighten your mood," Brother Hiruso said. He turned down a dark passage, the wheels bumping over an uneven section of stone. At the other end, light grew to reveal a vast, open courtyard containing the biggest vegetable patch Never had seen indoors. The patch, in turn, was lined with citrus trees and between them, evenly-spaced barrels for water and what seemed to be some manner of powdery growing-aid, based on the way monks spread it around the plants.

Other monks bent over the vegetables, placing braces of tomato or heads of spinach into woven baskets while others tended to the plants by checking the leaves for pests or sometimes the sturdiness of posts and string. Despite the size of the Divine Temple, which he was only able to make educated guesses at, the amount of produce that could be harvested was more than enough for the monks.

"You want to convince me that you care deeply for the people of the city because you feed some of them with this? Consider my mood lightened, like the very sun itself."

"No. Not to convince. Your understanding of what we do for those we must care for is quite immaterial," Hiruso said. "Instead, I want you to look – tell me, do they not seem at peace?"

"You want me to read minds now?"

"They are safe, and they take pride in their work. Worse

lives can be led."

"And how much of that safety is paid for by Ayuni's blood?"

Brother Hiruso gripped a handful of Never's hair with a hiss. "Fool! Close your mouth that you might still your words long enough to hear the truth. This," he waved his other hand at the garden, "could be her life, *that* is what I am offering should you reveal what you know. Ayuni could be free of her burdens. You hold that power."

"Only one person holds the blame for keeping her here for their personal gain – let's guess who, shall we?"

Hiruso backhanded Never, eyes blazing.

The blow split his lip. Blood filled his mouth and set his jaw to ringing, an ache spreading immediately. Still, it seemed the monk had held back.

Gasps rose from those nearest and workers stopped, looking up, faces confused or unnerved.

Never flashed a bloody grin at Hiruso. "Now, now, Brother. Let's not upset your happy little garden."

Hiruso wrenched the chair around and wheeled Never back into the dark corridor. "Your obstinate nature is growing most tiresome."

"Try sleeping strapped to a bed."

The monk stopped and walked around the chair to face Never, his jaw set. "I will not offer such leniency again."

"You would have me doom another to take her place."

"Ayuni has borne the burden long enough."

Never only shook his head. He stared back at the man in the dim light a long moment before answering. "You will have my reply in the morning," he said.

"I did not expect to wait."

"I only wish to give you enough time to produce the evidence I need."

"It is *I* that will be asking for evidence, Amouni."

"Yet all I can offer is my desire to protect Ayuni, wouldn't you say?" And it seemed that the man had already attempted to glean whatever he could via Never's blood. Perhaps that taught Hiruso that Snow was already dead?

It seemed the only reason Hiruso would attempt threats and coercion.

And still Never couldn't shake a lingering doubt; it badgered him each time Hiruso raised the possibility of more Amouni. Where did the man's certainty come from? Had Father said something? Lied to further his own cause? *That* seemed entirely possible. Perhaps Sikoka would know.

The monk folded his arms. "And your proof?"

"Send the Three Hammers to the capital – call them off, either that or show me that Ayuni and Muka are well."

Brother Hiruso moved back to take the handles on the back of Never's chair, resuming their walk.

"You have neither," Never said.

"Something which can be corrected at any time," the man replied. "But I will consider your request while you recall my promise. Ayuni freed from her burden, Muka lives and you are free to leave, all for the price of another sibling. By dawn, I will know everything and if I suspect a lie, you will be harvested to the very last drop."

***

When Sister Sikoka came once more to feed him, it was later than the previous evening. Full dark had fallen beyond the window of his cell – a well-appointed but still locked room. And as before, he had spent his time tied in place, which continued to drive home the notion that forced rest was not restful at all.

Despite the promise of possible escape, Never had fought against his bonds earlier but they were too comprehensive – severely limiting his movements. He might have bit his lip to get some blood flowing again, but without a cut on his captors, it was folly and he didn't believe crimson-fire was something he could *breathe*.

"I must be swift," Sister Sikoka said as she wheeled a trolley into the room, closing the door. A long black blanket covered the trolley, the material looked quite heavy.

"Did Ayuni send you?" Never asked.

Sikoka produced a knife and began slicing through the restraints. "And Mukatagami. Softly now."

He lowered his voice. "Are they safe?"

"As can be in these dark times – they will find you when we're done." She'd finished his legs and he flexed his muscles as she started on the straps binding his arms and torso.

"And what of you?" he asked.

"Carrying the dead is one of my duties and by the time anyone realises you are gone, I, too, will be away." She sawed through the final leather strap. "There."

He rose to a sitting position, a welcome freedom. "Carrying the dead?"

"Yes, all you have to do is lay still."

"I see." He hesitated. "Brother Hiruso strikes me as rather stubborn."

Sikoka shook her head as she lifted the sheet. "Don't worry for me, you just look after that girl."

He hoped she was right. "I will. What next?"

"You get beneath this blanket and I take you to the crematory. When you pass through, they will be waiting for you beyond the Harvest Garden."

He stretched across the trolley. "I hope you remembered to fire-proof this linen."

"The fires will not touch a hair on your head. Now hush."

She pushed him toward the door and he relaxed, forcing his breathing to remain shallow. Keeping him strapped down probably would have been better for achieving stillness but he didn't complain.

The wheels were smooth, barely a squeak as Sikoka wheeled him down the dim corridors. Several times, light bloomed beyond his blanket, but it did not last; it seemed few lamps were lit of an evening. Once, she offered a greeting to someone, who returned it softly, but the trolley did not stop.

The hum of many voices soon grew louder and beneath it, the click of wood against wood, providing the rhythm to what was some manner of wordless song. A celebratory tone suggested a happy moment.

Sister Sikoka came to a halt when they reached a point where the song grew so loud that it became clear the trolley was now adjacent from whatever was occurring. A celebration or ceremony? Never ignored an itch on his forearm. They were obviously close enough to be seen by those within, yet hopefully whatever was happening was too sacred for wandering gazes, a possibility suggested by Sikoka coming to a halt.

The echo spoke of a vast room of stone and as the song faded away, the sound of soft-clad footfalls filled a reverent hush, the swish of many robes going with it. When that eased, the faint crackle of flame, as from across a hall, took its place.

Brother Hiruso's voice rang out, resonant with paternal warmth. "We welcome you, former Acolytes, to the midnight hour and the first moments of a new day, the first moments of your rebirth as full Brothers and Sisters of the Phoenix." A long pause followed. "Now, remove your collars, those which have served you throughout each year of your preparation, and cast them into the fire."

More swishing of robes and a change in the crackle of flames.

"May the Phoenix watch over you as you watch over the people of Kiymako," Hiruso said.

A cheer rose and then the rest of the crowd joined it – a fair number by the volume, and Sikoka started the trolley moving once more. The song receded and when she had to stop and lift the trolley to navigate a particularly narrow turn, she spoke.

"I had hoped to miss the ceremony, but it seemed we nattered on too much."

"Will Hiruso send someone after us?" He kept his voice soft.

"If he does, it won't be at once. His duties extend into the morning; he will stay and speak with each new Brother and Sister about their First Pledge."

"Giving us how much time?"

"He will finish before dawn."

"And now?"

"A little ways further to the crematory."

Sister Sikoka encountered no-one else in the quiet halls

and at one point she picked up speed, wheels rattling.

"Ah...?"

"Hush. I just need to build up a little momentum."

The trolley hit an incline and Never gripped the edges until Sikoka reached level ground again, and then she let the trolley roll to a halt, her footfalls moving around to stop nearby. Next, a thumping against wood.

The squeak of a door opening followed instantly.

"What took so long?" a wheezing voice asked; an elderly man.

"Ceremony," Sikoka said.

"Hurry it along then – and you might as well get up, lad."

The blanket was drawn free and Never rose.

A large chamber of stone, filled with the scents of smoke and pine. Empty coffins lined one wall and a long bench covered in powder-filled jars stood adjacent to a gaping maw of blackened stone; the crematory.

As Never had surmised, an elderly monk stood beside Sister Sikoka. He was frowning. "So, you're the one we're going to all this trouble for then? You're Ayuni's brother?"

"I am." Never hopped down. "And speaking of trouble, just how do you both plan on getting away with this?"

"I told you, Never," Sikoka said. "I am leaving as soon as you do – via a different path. I would take Okan with me, but he refuses."

The man waved a hand. "I'm not one for flights into the night. If Brother Pewu takes issue with my role here then I will meet whatever fate he wishes; *he* is still Head of the Temple, not that snake Hiruso."

Never stared at them both. "I'm sure we could help you escape if—"

"Enough dallying," Sister Sikoka said. "You need to leave now to be certain, all you have to do is slide down the chute within. Okan will open the hatch where you will find yourself in the Harvest Garden. I trust you can deal with the outer walls yourself?"

He sighed. "I cannot force you, so accept my prayers to Pacela for your safety."

"We will," Sikoka said.

Never climbed into the mouth, the scent of char so much stronger now. He crawled forward but Sikoka called to him. "Never, please send Ayuni my love." Her voice was a little husky. "Tell her not to worry about me; I have a few friends left."

"I will." And hopefully she was right; and more, that such friends were powerful or crafty indeed.

A grinding followed, revealing a pale glow ahead. He continued on, hands and knees quickly covered in soot – soot that was once flesh, bone and pine. In the dark, he couldn't discern where the flames would have entered the stone tunnel, but when the floor started to slope down the glow became a strong slither of moonlight.

He twisted as best he could in the cramped confines so that he would slide feet-first, then pushed himself forward. The bumps and scrapes to his backside and elbows were a small price to pay compared to the condition people usually found themselves in when they took the chute.

Light grew quickly – the bottom rushed up and he thumped into a huge pile of ashes, clouds puffing up to choke him. He coughed, climbing free and blinking away the ash of the chute's last visitors.

He glanced back up with a frown. "A warning would

have been welcome, Sister."

Still, there was no time to tarry. The chute had dumped him in a small garden where half a dozen markers stood in a sparse grove. Most were stone, shaped as the Phoenix, though two were made of wood – one so old and faded that no markings were present. Grave markers?

He paused to listen; only the sound of his own breathing.

No hint of movement anywhere in the night, beyond the trees or the wall as best he could tell. Clouds were slowly covering the moon, darkening the temple and the garden too, the shadow creeping to cover a wooden gate and then the trees and finally the markers.

It seemed the perfect time to leave... but he freed his wings only to pause once more. What if the Hammers were lying in wait? They'd certainly captured him easily enough before.

"You can't wait forever, fool." Never ran for the wall, slipping between a pair of juniper where he launched himself into the air.

Chapter 30

Never wheeled high above the temple.

The night air was cool, welcome after being covered first in a heavy blanket and then covered in the ash of human remains. The act of flying itself was just as welcome, especially when compared to the subtler joys of being drugged and strapped to a bed.

Below, the dark of the forest was complete, yet he was still able to catch a glimpse of flashing light – someone holding a mirror to the half-seen moon? He swooped closer and smiled; two figures stood in a small clearing before the temple walls near the garden, one taller than the other.

Muka and Ayuni.

He landed easily, still smiling. "Sorry to be so tardy."

Ayuni ran forward to hug him, squeezing. "Never."

Never hugged her back – clenching his jaw as a wave of protectiveness washed over him. Hiruso's knives would not touch her ever again. Ayuni *had* to be protected, no matter the cost. She deserved the chance to reclaim everything the Temple had stolen – her freedom, her family, her life.

"Into the trees," Muka said, waving them into single-file.

Once they were out of sight, Muka slowed. "I'm glad to see you in one piece," he said as he led them along a path, seemingly by memory, since there was so little light. "We've camped on the outskirts of Yalinamo so it's going to take a while. Keep an ear out for anything unnatural."

"Are you both well?" Never asked.

"We are," Ayuni said. "Between the charm and your appearances, the journey was easy enough."

"Good," Never said, then fell silent to focus on their surroundings, lit by patches of moonlight as often as not. But even with the sometime-light, he saw no evidence of homes despite how close they must have passed to some of them, Muka's trail winding and thin since he occasionally caught a foot on undergrowth or tree roots.

When they finally reached the camp, dawn was breaking. Muka paused to crouch within the tree line, where beyond, a decaying shack waited in a clearing; it was little more than a smudge of pale timber. Long-since abandoned, it seemed devoid of life. Maybe it was, maybe it wasn't – again, Never couldn't shake the feeling that the Hammers might be watching or waiting. Was that simply worry born of his previous failure? They'd been so damn quiet, he'd been lucky to sense them the first time.

"Think it's safe?" he asked.

"Let's wait a moment longer," Ayuni replied.

Never strained his ears, closing his eyes, but heard nothing. At a hint of movement, he tensed – small golden circles appeared on the tree beside him, like that of a huge moth. Only the shape made no sound. The eyes – if that was what they were – regarded him, tilted to one side... as if questioning.

"Muka?" Never kept his voice low.

The man gave a soft chuckle. "It is only a hin, Never. Do not startle it, perhaps it can help us."

The glow flared a little, still not enough to give their position away. "How?"

"Simply ask, it will understand."

"And the price?" Never asked. "My *lunai*?"

"Only if it returns, best not to give a *hin* too much before it has proven itself. Some are quite fickle."

"Very well." He looked back to the small creature. "Hin, can you scout the area? Are we the only people nearby?"

The golden orbs blinked, and it fluttered from the trunk, quickly disappearing into the darkness.

"How long will we have to wait?" he asked.

"The fae can be quite swift," Ayuni said.

Never nodded, leaning against the tree. Yet they did not have to wait long, as the creature reappeared, hovering before him. "Are we alone?" he whispered.

The orbs blinked twice, which Never took to mean 'yes'.

"And how do I repay it?"

"Touching the *hin* is usually enough," Muka said. "It will be a faint sensation, only."

Never lifted a hand.

The moth-like creature alighted on his palm, tiny feet exploring his skin, seeming to quest for the old scratch. As it did, the sensation of an almost negligible amount of his vitality leaving. Then the *hin* flickered and disappeared.

He shook his head, half in disbelief. "I guess we're safe to go," he said as he started across the clearing, a hand on one of his knives despite the hin's report. At the door he paused, resting fingertips against the worn wood. Still nothing. He pushed, then slipped inside but found only two packs on the floor, other details lost in the darkness. "Well then, fine work from our tiny scout."

Ayuni smiled. "They can be truly impressive."

"We shouldn't risk a light," Muka said as he followed Ayuni, sheathing his tyrant. "So it's a cold meal for now."

"I'd rather it be cold and be able to feed myself," Never said.

"What do you mean?" Ayuni asked. She moved to one of the packs and began removing flatbread and fruit.

"Sister Sikoka had to feed me while I was imprisoned," he said. "She sends her love."

Ayuni straightened. "Then she's safe? When her messenger reached us I didn't know what to think..."

"She told me she had friends that could help her; she seemed confident."

Ayuni nodded, a slight smile on her face. "That's how she is. I think that maybe even Brother Hiruso would have trouble finding her if she did manage to get away... I'd hoped to see her again but perhaps it's safer not to have tried. I guess she knew that."

"Speaking of being found, what happened to you, Never?" Muka asked. "Our path here was calm enough. We assumed that the plan had worked."

"It did at first," Never said, explaining the stir he'd created in the first two towns. "But in Okana I was ambushed – I heard them, but I was still too slow, the net was upon me and before I could cut my way free, they'd used a drug. It had to be the Hammers."

"And they took you to the temple?" Ayuni asked.

"Hiruso performed a few tests on my blood. He's convinced that Father sired more children and I let him believe I knew of one but Sikoka freed me before our standoff could go any further."

Ayuni's expression darkened. "He took your blood?"

"Yes. To see if its healing powers are like yours. He said it was not as potent but during our discussion he gave something away. I know his fear; it is the oldest fear. He cannot bear to die, no matter how the Temple heals with what it learns from your blood. That is his true goal, to reclaim his youth. Perhaps that is part of the secret behind his strength."

Muka was nodding. "It would explain some of his power, though just as much comes from his *lunai* as head of the Temple."

"I wonder, does that extend to sensing Amouni blood? Wanatek inferred as much once. And Hiruso did meet me when I landed east of Najin. Part of me wonders if the charm did more than we gave it credit for?"

"I doubt it is so powerful, if Hiruso can sense you," Muka said.

"But neither he nor the Hammers found us," Never replied. "It wasn't until we separated that I was taken, and I don't believe the Hammers could have guessed which towns we'd chosen."

Ayuni handed over sliced strawberries in the thin bread. "And none would be as fast as your wings."

Muka frowned in the growing light. "If Hiruso had been able to pinpoint your location and the charm has foiled him thus far, then I doubt we ought to split up again."

"It would support his request for the Temples to search

for us, and the releasing of the Hammers," Never added.

"That doesn't mean we can't be followed by conventional means," Ayuni said. "All will know we are here in Yalinamo."

"Perhaps we aren't the only ones being hunted?" Never said. "I came across Wanatek in Okana, he was meeting someone – a woman on the outskirts of town."

Muka straightened. "Was he detained? Did you speak with him?"

Never shook his head. "I didn't want to risk drawing attention on him; I can only assume he is well. He wasn't alone, Etsu was with him. Something is afoot in Najin?"

"Yes, but as before I will not reveal it now – save to say that should we survive our task here, I hope you will see a different Najin upon your return."

"As do I," Never said.

"What now?" Ayuni asked.

"I'd love some sleep," Never replied. "Can we afford until mid-morning?"

Muka nodded. "Probably. All the temples already know to watch for us, so we can't exactly outrun word of your escape anyway."

"We can watch and prepare," Ayuni added. "Though I'm not sure what our next step should be."

"I think we have to trust the charm and rely on stealth or speed," Never said. "How far to your village?"

"Three days to the feet of the Cesanha Mountains," she said. "But my village, I don't remember exactly. It seemed halfway up the range. I'm sorry, I was so young."

Never took a bite. Not bad. "So, boldly or quietly with our charm?"

"Meaning?" Muka asked.

"Should we travel as Monks of the Temple or something more unassuming?"

"I think the risk is the same, no matter what," Ayuni said.

"Still have those disguises?" he asked Muka.

"We do."

"Then wake me when it's time. I think we deserve a chance to show off the hard work your fellow rebels put into those robes."

Chapter 31

The Beshano River churned white before him, tumbling over jagged rocks in a constant spray, while a little ways upstream it was a smooth pool before plummeting down a short fall. A solid-looking bridge waited beneath it, one side half-covered in a mist that even now drifted across to cool his face beneath the rising sun.

"The Bridge of Mist – we'll reach the foothills by evening." Muka stood nearby, arms folded over the flame symbol on his chest – but he appeared impressed rather than disappointed. "Perhaps I misjudged just how potent the charm is," he said, a trace of what seemed to be pride in his voice.

"It has been an easy enough passage so far," Ayuni said. She was a little way across the bridge, her hand outstretched to touch the mist. Unlike Muka and Never, she hadn't really needed a disguise since her robe was already cut from temple cloth.

"I could even think it was too easy," Never observed. He turned to face their back trail. The only figure on the road, dwindling from sight now, was an old woman and a boy in a wagon, who'd shared news of a quiet path ahead.

"Do you expect ambush?" Muka asked.

He shrugged. "We have to, don't we? Hiruso would have learnt of my escape quite swiftly; he would have men all over the forest, but we've encountered few who gave us even a second look."

"If he can trace your progress then an ambush may wait ahead but doesn't all evidence point toward the *yochan-fang* clouding his vision? Why not strike sooner, closer to Yalinamo and the Temple?"

Ayuni returned. "Unless he's busy chasing Sikoka?"

"We'd be his first target," Muka said. "There is a chance she has slipped away in the chaos that we doubtlessly left in our wake."

She nodded. "I hope so."

"Then he has yet to reveal his hand or the charm is a miracle," Never said. "Or both. So either way, let's keep our wits about us."

The span was broad enough for wagons to pass but not so long, they were soon on the far bank starting along the road.

Master!

The voice rang in his mind and he spun.

Standing within the rapids, white water doing nothing whatsoever to stir long folds of pale green robes, was a guide. Its bare arms were outstretched, and the fish head glistened in the light.

"By the Phoenix," Ayuni breathed, her words nearly lost beneath the rasp of steel as Muka drew his *sisan*.

"It is well," Never told them, approaching the guide, stopping at the water's edge. "Guide. What do you want?"

We have been searching for you. You must save the Forge. It is urgent.

Never frowned. No guide had seemed so agitated before. "The Forge?"

Where you have always been; the Covenant requires you preserve it or all will be lost. So you told us, Master.

Did it mean Father? Snow? Someone else, someone older? Unlike some Guides, this one appeared fully present in the world. And unlike the mostly toneless voices, there seemed to be a fear to its words.

Muka stepped closer. "Never, what is happening?"

"This is an ancient Amouni guide. I believe their purpose was to both preserve knowledge and assist in travelling to places usually reserved for Amouni. It wants me to save something called the Forge."

"What does that mean?" Ayuni asked.

"I have no idea... but there's a chance Father may have used it here in Kiymako."

Her eyes widened. "Father? Here?"

Master.

He ignored the Guide. "I think we should follow it. Aside from my own curiosity, there's a chance Father left something behind that could help against Hiruso."

"I would like to see this Forge too," Ayuni said.

Muka sheathed his blade, scratching at stubble on his cheek. "Is there any danger?"

"Possibly, but I have visited several such Amouni sites and had no trouble," Never said. Aside from the Guardians in the sky, but that was different. If the Guide was going to take them somewhere similar to the Preparation Chamber, surely there was little to fear? He faced the Guide again. "We must all travel there, Guide."

So it shall be. Two more arms appeared from the robes. *Do not release my hand.*

"Take a hand but don't let go," Never said. "It's a little disconcerting, quite fast. You'll probably see some strange lights but just remember, don't let go. We'll likely surface in a tiled room."

"You mean, we're travelling in the river?" Muka asked. His brow had drawn together now.

"In a fashion, I suppose we will. Ready?" Never waited for them both to nod. Where Muka didn't appear too thrilled, Ayuni's expression was one of determination.

Never reached out and gripped the cool hand.

The Guide waited for Muka and Ayuni, then began to sink.

"Won't the rocks –" Muka's voice was interrupted by a void of dark water as the Guide pulled them under. Lights of vivid green and blue began to streak by, hurtling along beside them. Some twisted and jumped about and they eventually blurred together, giving the sense of vast speed – disconcerting since to Never, it felt as though his body remained motionless.

When they slowed and faded into darkness, the Guide spoke once more.

The Vestibule will be attended.

By now, the words seemed almost ritualistic, since like before, there didn't seem to be an attendant anymore. Never found himself standing in a tiled chamber of red and white, the pattern difficult to trace.

"I'm dry," Ayuni said from behind him, incredulity in her voice.

"Me too," Muka added.

Never nodded as he moved to a nearby podium. He ran his hands across the wall behind it until he found the tile that depressed with a soft click. A silver light appeared in the shape of a door, sliding open to reveal a long corridor. Pale light waited at its end.

"In we go then," Never said.

The room at the end of the corridor spread in a wide, domed chamber. It was lined with tables, stools and cabinets, along with all manner of objects he could not name. Many were crafted from silver or steel, as tall or taller than he. Some were stout chests on wheels with an odd assortment of handles. Yet more pieces appeared as fence posts with thin wire stretched between them in triangles; there were also an assortment of weapons beneath clear quartz – much like the blades found in the Amouni ruin beneath the Folhan Ranges, but axes and bows too. Muka had gone to examine them, eyes alight with interest.

"Be thankful they are locked away," Never said. "The last pair I saw claimed the souls of those who wielded them."

Muka nodded solemnly and moved on to a thing that seemed to be a hoe connected to wheels, hands at his sides. Ayuni was similarly enthralled by a series of paintings adorning one wall – far across the chamber. The details were difficult to make out from a distance. He didn't join her yet; a frown had formed. Had Father truly been here?

He drifted toward a series of books that lay open on one of the tables, each bound in old leather. He lifted the first; a series of numbers and letters written in precise Marlosi. Meaningless. But the second book was more interesting, a journal open to a final entry – Amouni words seemed to sear into his mind as he read, the unfamiliar and familiar as one, and the more he studied them the clearer the account became:

I will meet with the Old Wolf for the last time, it seems. He has requested the Sparrow's Solace due to its proximity, I suspect. By now he is surely far too ancient to help; he always claims to have known a time before even the Bleak Man, but I have no other choice. If he can only remember just one more clue, it will be enough – I am so close.

The wolfman from the vision – it had to be Father's writings, the man had been here! Never flipped back a page, a single line only:

Yet another failure. There is something wrong with these servant-women.

He gripped the book, hard, turning the pages more swiftly now, skimming over more reports of failures of 'servant-women' to bear children. He also flipped by other failures – and successes – of varying natures; research into Amouni language, healing and locations of ruins, names he did not recognise until he reached the first page where the only entry was a year.

More journals waited before Never. He lifted several, checking each year until he found one that seemed old enough. His hands were shaking as he started turning the pages – until the word Quisoa leapt forth.

I have seen the Quisoan woman again; Jenisa. She is fetching in so many ways, tender but fierce, the conquest has been its own pleasure truly, but most thrilling – her pregnancy is progressing further than any since the whore in the islands. Jenisa will bear fruit; I am certain of it, she is strong enough!

Never trembled. His father was every bit the fiend Snow had claimed. Every speck of the man was *filth*. Yet to see Mother's name written; how beautiful. The brief ring of her voice, humming, seemed to echo in his mind, soothing the building rage.

On the next page, another single line – this one near to gouging the parchment.

Success! The Amouni line of Ascended will live on!

He turned another page for a longer entry – only for a flat, emotionless voice to interrupt.

Master, the fuel you have generously provided is ready. We require your aid now.

Never's head snapped up. A figure in purple robes stood before him. Her arms were bare and her head that of a serpent, flat grey eyes regarding him. Beyond the figure, an empty chamber only.

He dropped the journal and dashed several steps across the room. "Ayuni? Muka?"

Only the echo of his voice returned.

"Where are they?" Never roared.

Being prepared.

"Prepared?"

Of course. We called, and you came with fuel for the Forge, as you have always promised.

No use arguing with it. "Take me to the Forge."

Yes, Master.

The serpent-woman glided across the chamber, heading for one of the paintings – a tall portrait of an Ascended Amouni. The figure bore radiant golden wings where she stood, her pale robe bearing the five-pointed leaf but more, a twin set of eyes on each shoulder. Her expression was haughty, a touch of scorn in her eye. The artist had rendered her well – was she Father's fantasy or a real figure?

The Guide touched the frame and it slid aside soundlessly, revealing a short passage and a well-lit room beyond, sunlight streaming within. He strode forward; pushing past the Guide, who offered no protest.

The Forge was unlike any he'd seen before.

A giant bowl of dusky quartz dominated an otherwise empty room, reflecting the skylight, broad enough to contain an entire pond. At its base, a spout lay poised above a long trough lined with silver and marked with unfamiliar Amouni runes. A chill crept across Never as he approached. "Where are they?"

Within, as instructed. We shall call the fire now, so you can add your blood. A different, similar guide stood by a panel on the opposite wall, pressing down as it spoke.

Never whirled back to the quartz. "No!"

Master?

Above, the roof was shimmering, becoming mirror-like – yet it was no mere mirror; it seemed to hold the light, as if storing up the sun. Heat built, beaming down on the bowl.

"Stop this."

The Forge cannot be unlit.

Never threw his cloak back and let his wings burst free as he leapt up. It only took two beats of his wings to clear the rim. Within, two figures floated in a glittering pool of water – Ayuni and Muka. Their faces were calm, but they did not move, did not react to the growing heat that even now seemed to be singeing his very wings. Were they still alive?

He swooped over the surface and reached into the water, taking Ayuni by the shoulders. The water was already warm and it seemed to cling to his skin. He pulled her free, setting her down on the stone floor. Then he leapt up again and lifted Muka out with a grunt, expending no small effort to do so.

There, he checked upon them both; faint evidence of their life was clear in the gentle rise and fall of their chests. He stood, turning on the guides. Both waited together now, both in shades of purple and wearing snake-heads. "What have you done to them?"

Only as instructed. They have been placed in a deep sleep to await a higher use – they always struggle less this way. He could not tell which had answered.

"Being boiled down to slush?"

The Forge must not fail; you have warned us about such a tragedy.

"Remind me."

It must be provided with new materials at regular intervals else it loses all potency. Your absence has been significant, and your orders made it very clear what we must do.

"And the purpose."

To render unique offerings down to their unique qualities. One gestured. *It isolates and extracts.*

The second nodded its snake-head. *It can also be used to remove undesired attributes. It is one companion to the Hor Pyrilh.*

One? How many existed? *Hor Pyrilh* – The Human Maps, a terrifying tome. Just where had Snow taken his copy from – not here. The archive Father had written about? "Where is the book now?"

You have taken it with you.

Good enough, perhaps. "We are leaving, wait for me at the podium," Never commanded.

Yes, Master.

He sat between Ayuni and Muka, leaning back against the trough. The sound of their breathing was faint but steady enough. He tried shaking each gently, calling their names but nothing woke them. Would time be enough? Calling the Guides might have worked but could they truly be trusted?

Perhaps he had to – he wasn't getting anywhere by himself.

"Guide, wake them."

A purple figure appeared. *Yes, Master.* It did not speak again but after a moment it flickered from sight.

"Never?"

Never turned.

Ayuni was rising, frowning as she rubbed at her temples. "What happened?"

"The Guides were a little overzealous," he said. "How do you feel?"

"Not quite myself somehow. Or maybe just a little unwell, I don't know how to explain it."

Muka stirred next. When he rose, it was with a muttering. "One of those things... where are we?" He glanced around, staring up at the quartz.

"In a chamber that Father used for unpleasant things –

but I think we need to leave now, just to be safe. Can you both stand? How do you feel?" he asked Muka.

Ayuni stood slowly, Muka following. The warrior stretched his limbs and flexed his fingers. "Well enough."

"Good."

Never led them back into the main chamber, where he paused before his father's journals. Taking them was a risk. They'd probably end up dry after the passage in the river, but once beyond the confines of the Amouni stronghold could they fall into the wrong hands? Could they somehow be used against him?

If he left them behind, the journals could be found again quite easily – Never had an inkling as to where he stood, and if he was wrong, all he had to do was travel to the Beshano River and call a Guide.

"Never?" Ayuni stood beside him.

"I fear what these journals contain – this entire room," he said. "But it may include writings about his time with your mother. Do you want to search before we leave?"

She stared down at the journals a long moment before shaking her head. "Not today."

"Truly?"

She smiled up at him. "I want to find my mother, not my father."

"Are you certain?"

"Never, please trust me. Finding Mother is more important than unearthing his ghost, considering what I was to him."

Was she hiding her true feelings? Not that he doubted Ayuni's sincerity to find her mother, and he could well-understand her need, but was it a brave front? There'd been true betrayal on her face when she'd realised what Father had expected of her. Or perhaps Never was pushing his own weakness onto his sister? His own need to learn more about the man who'd provided so little, shouldn't have mattered so.

He had to place Ayuni first.

"We should leave," Muka said, breaking the quiet.

Never shook his head. He hadn't actually answered her. "I believe we are beneath the strange dome near the trading corral, if you ever change your mind, since I don't wish to take the books."

"No. Let's finish our journey," she said.

"Very well, let's return to the mountains." He started across the stone. The journals were safe and he could return himself at any time – in fact, the moment he knew Ayuni was free from the Temple he would do exactly that.

She was his priority now.

"Will the Guides be a problem?" Muka asked. "After all, they seemed to act on their own before."

Never shook his head. "Not if I have anything to say about it."

Chapter 32

The road leading up into the Cesanha Mountains ran straight and broad, a steady incline, lined by towering green pine trees whose needles were stirred by a chill evening wind that cut across the path.

"We should make camp, darkness will come swiftly here," Muka said.

They found a suitable grove and set up camp, eating quietly before splitting the watch – Never took the first shift.

The crackle of their tiny fire was muted where it burned fitfully in the pit, the even breathing of Ayuni and Muka faint beneath it. From his position on a rock, moonlight offered some detail to the woods, broad trunks and low-hanging branches – where he saw a small figure flitting along.

He reached for a blade, but it was only the *hin* with its golden glowing eyes – only now it scampered forward on all fours, appearing more like a small animal rather than a moth. When it drew close enough, its leaf-like skin became clear, gleaming beneath the moon. The golden eyes appeared larger too, especially in a face without discernible nose or mouth – yet it extended stalk-like fingers, petals drifting down to the ground as it did.

He frowned at it, why had the *hin* grown larger since last he saw it? Or perhaps it had grown twice already. After all, hadn't the butterfly in Tisura been green, with two yellow markings? And like the moth, it had seemed attracted to his blood.

"Slow down, fellow," he said softly.

The *hin* retracted its arm, sitting back on its haunches.

"We've a contract, right?"

It nodded, a solemn movement.

"Then let's see what you can do once more, little scout. I want to know who is nearby, if anyone follows us. Can you do that?"

Another nod, more vigorous this time.

"Thank you – as fast as you can."

The *hin* spun, barely stirring the leaves as it charged back into the woods. Never stared after the creature. Perhaps his blood had changed it, like it seemed to change everything else it encountered. The question was just how much and in what way?

By the time the *hin* returned, his watch was nearing an end.

"What did you find?"

The creature nodded, then raised both forearms, holding up first eight fingers and then ten. Next, it swung an arm sharply, single finger extended.

"Eighteen monks, all armed?"

A nod.

"Following us?"

The *hin* shook its head. Then it closed its eyes, tilted its head to the side and rested both hands beneath.

The monks were sleeping – good news at least. "How close are they?"

It shrugged, then blinked a few times.

Never tried again. "This side of the Beshano River?"

Now the *hin* nodded.

"And this side of the forked road where a tree has been struck by lightning?"

The fae creature gave a tiny jump with its nod.

"Thank you," he said. They were still a day behind and according to Ayuni's estimation, her village was near the same distance further up the mountain. Still, eighteen monks, while a formidable force itself, hardly made it seem as though Hiruso was worried. Why not send the Hammers? After all, they'd captured Never once already.

The *hin* was beginning to twitch.

"Sorry." Never drew a blade and pricked the point of his thumb. Blood welled, and he held his hand out. The *hin* approached, its own plant-like fingers outstretched, then latched on to him.

The *hin* drew his blood forth this time, golden eyes glowing brighter.

Never pulled away after just a moment, not wanting to give it too much. In the scheme of things, it was hardly an amount to concern Never – but there was always a chance it would somehow hurt the hin. Simply because nothing bad had happened to the creature *yet* did not prove nothing *would*.

"Want another task?" he asked.

The *hin* gave another bounce.

"Good. I want you to slow the monks down somehow."

It blinked.

"Hmmm..." He paused to think. Could a *hin* influence the very forest? "Would the trees help you close or move the trail if you asked?"

The *hin* clapped its hands together then once again disappeared.

Would it be successful? Even a slight delay might make enough difference between recapture and escape. At least the monks were asleep. "As I ought to be." Never woke Muka, explaining about the hin, then sought his own bedding.

At dawn he nearly sprang from his bedroll when Ayuni called his name; he'd slept far deeper than usual but rising was no chore. "So, this is what a truly restful sleep feels like – I think I'd forgotten," he said, squinting against the rising sun. His rest suggested that at least one part of him felt that the *hin* had successfully delayed pursuit.

They set out to climb once more, with Ayuni mostly quiet, her attention fixed on her surroundings. Occasionally, she'd shake her head. "So little is familiar but it *feels* right nevertheless."

"Trust your instincts," Never would say, and they'd follow whatever path she chose – not all of which were well-maintained, and a few turned out to be dead ends. But by noon they crested a hill that looked down upon a wide green vale and caused Ayuni to come to a halt.

In its centre lay a wide platform that covered enough ground to stand in for a village, yet there were no buildings upon it and the boards seemed to have been built upon giant, shorn tree trunks. Instead, strange ruins littered the place – once brightly-coloured tents and pavilions, now pale echoes only of their former cheer, low steel fences surrounding nothing but debris and mighty cages gone to rust.

"I know this valley," Ayuni said.

"As do I," Muka added. "It was called the Vale of Lights, a place where travelling performers came from all corners. Only the most famous singers, musicians, *rudama* and acrobats would visit. As a child, I once saw a woman shatter glass with only her voice."

"Ayuni?" Never asked.

She was nodding. "Let's go down; there's something here."

Chapter 33

Never paused to look up at the wide stair that had been cut from one of the trunks.

The fallen tree was one of many that made up the support for the village-sized platform above, every trunk at least half again as tall as he. Between each one rested huge wedges to prevent movement, though the floor of the valley was level. The butts of the trunks had been worn down by wind, rain and forgotten saw marks; he rested a hand against the one that had the stair cut within. "Who made this place?"

"Supposedly the Divine Throne did," Muka said. "A century ago at least, and now probably a decade since it was used. The performers stopped coming after a disastrous storm as they considered it an ill omen."

Ayuni was already climbing the steps. Never hurried after her, Muka close behind.

Wind carried the scent of stagnant water across the vast platform, and with it, the dull sound of torn canvas snapping. Ayuni had paused at the nearest ring of steel posts, running her fingers across the chain link, where once rope must have stretched.

"I have definitely been here. There was laughter and light and music. I remember gasps of awe too... and darkness on our way. Or as we left?" Her expression softened. "I can almost see the performers and their costumes again. They seemed so glamorous; I wanted to be like them, to travel and see the land."

"Then we are on the right track," Never said.

"I'm sure of it."

She led them across the boards, which barely creaked beneath their feet despite their faded colour. A circular tent of leeched blue, half in tatters, stood nearby, tall letters painted on its side. It seemed most were missing, but it was enough for Muka to identify the tent as that of a painter. "When I visited, the man within was painting a horse with wings... it slept within a field of golden grass."

Ayuni pointed to the next decaying tent as they neared, this one much larger. Part of the roof sagged with standing water. "What of this one, Muka? I seem to remember one of the red tents had animals?"

"I think so, yes."

Inside was only the skeletal remains of a pen, not even the hint of straw or even ancient droppings. The central column had been scratched but Never found the marks to be old when he bent to examine them.

The next pavilion had kept far more of its canvas; a bird exploded from the corner, feathers drifted from the nest. It clung to the edge of the roofing and looked down at them, beak snapping as it chirped.

"Forgive us," Never said, sweeping a bow.

Similar scenes were repeated as they drew closer to the

main pavilion, which had borne the brunt of time better than other tents. It concealed something of an arena, the ghosts of raised seating encircled a clear floor littered with debris now, but which must have once been the focus point. Of the chairs that remained, all were rotten or broken, some little more than kindling. Vandals or folks desperate for firewood in cold times?

Here, the central column helped support the roof. Birds still roosted high above, their... gifts clear in piles across the floor. Yet something shone in the light. "I see something," he said, approaching the gleaming object.

It was long and thin... a silver cane. Something of such value would hardly have remained in plain sight for so long. He slowed as he neared it; the floor around was littered with writings. Some in faded paint, some that might have even been blood and yet other words had been scorched into the very wood. The writing was hard, jagged, writ large too.

He bent down, hand outstretched.

"Best not to touch it," Muka said.

Never stopped. "Is it cursed then?"

"So say the words around it, yes," he replied.

Ayuni's eyes were a little wide as she read. "Is this the cane carried by the Master of the Vale? The man who betrayed the performers?"

"Yes." Muka folded his arms as he spoke. "During a great storm that claimed the lives of many, it is said he ran forth – releasing pegs and lashings, driving animals free and calling the lightning down upon the Vale. Supposedly, he was *rudama* and could have eased the storm but instead, he fanned the flames. None know why."

"No wonder it has not been touched."

"They say his stomach was filled with stones and his body buried headfirst."

Never shook his head. "Well, enough of that delightful history lesson perhaps. Ayuni, you said you had been here. Is it possible your village lies beyond the valley, higher in the mountains?"

"I believe so."

"Then we'll have to find a trail somewhere."

"I remember darkness – but it didn't seem to be night," she said with a nod, gaze caught in a far-off place. "And before we reached this place the light was so sudden and so bright. It hurt my eyes... I think there was a cave or a tunnel."

"Then let's keep going," Never said.

Outside, the abandonment continued until only a handful of tents remained between them and the edge of the giant platform. Beyond it in turn waited dense forest creeping across the empty space, animal trails visible at its edges but nothing that screamed 'main road' or 'highway'.

"I suppose one is as good as any other," he said. "So long as it's near the next set of steps. They must be a little farther—"

"Wait," Ayuni said. She was staring at one of the sagging tents – it might have once been a bright yellow, but it was a poor reflection of its former self now. Nothing about it seemed distinctive, compared to any other. It had a little less canvas perhaps.

Never rejoined her.

"This one is familiar." She led them across the floorboards and inside, revealing a typical pile of debris, wood, steel and rotting ropes. Again, nothing to separate it from any other tent. She pointed to the mess in the corner. "Can we move that?"

"Of course." Never set to work, joined by Muka and Ayuni, and in short order they had cleared the floor. It was grimy, slick with the rot, a darker shade than the rest of the flooring.

Ayuni was pacing, muttering to herself about a 'trigger'. Finally, she stopped and moved to a spot beside the newly revealed floor. Once there, she clasped her hands together and closed her eyes, as if in prayer. She took a single step to her left then, and stomped her foot down, hard.

Something clicked.

A trap door had popped open – it rested within the floor where space had been cleared.

Ayuni beamed over at them. "I knew it!"

"This leads to your village?" Never asked.

"I think so. Now that I'm here I'm remembering... the tunnel is below the Vale and we used it only when the travellers were here. I think it leads up into the mountain, to my village."

"I hope it wasn't the only way in or out," Never said, "since it obviously hasn't been used for a long time."

She paused. "No, I believe there was another way... a river? I think Mother and I used to wait at the water's edge for a raft. It's hard to be sure, but I know we'll find her there."

Never exchanged a glance with Muka, whose expression was hardly a mirror of Ayuni's hope and confidence.

"I saw that," she told them. "And I have faith, so you have to as well."

"We have faith in you, Ayuni," Muka said.

Never nodded.

"Then let's get moving," she said, her smile just as bright as before.

Chapter 34

After closing the trap door behind them, they started down a dark tunnel. The passage was as well-constructed as it was long – after a series of wooden supports gave way to carven stone walls, Never began to wonder whether the entry point at the Vale of Lights was actually the original end point of the tunnel?

But more important for now was *their* destination. It was becoming increasingly likely that Ayuni's village did wait at the end of the steadily rising passage, or at least a place that had been made by human hands.

Very occasionally they passed skylights set high above; these seemed to be open to the elements but were too narrow for any to climb down. What little light they provided was enough to drink from their flasks and move on, once more needing to rely on the single lantern Muka carried. By the fourth such patch of light it was clear the afternoon was wearing on, but here was a point where the slope became steps.

And again, well-crafted.

Never couldn't help wondering about the possible Amouni influence on the island – they had been everywhere else, it seemed – but simply because it was old and built to last did not make it Amouni. The stair still seemed ancient at least. It was wide enough for four to walk and regular landings provided moments for rest.

When it finally came to an end at a wide door of stone, Never discarded his theory of the Amouni. Kiymako writing spread across the sealed door.

Ayuni ran her hands across the chiselled words. "It says 'to those who seek to pass beyond this point know that a pure heart has naught to fear'."

"I might not be welcome then," Never said.

Ayuni waved a hand at him. "You'll be fine – we all will, but only if we can open it."

"Any memories?" Muka asked.

She shook her head.

Muka rested the lantern against the door and began to search his pack for his flask. Never rubbed at his neck. "I assume it's not going to be a simple matter of pushing or pulling. No handle, no levers on the wall, no panels, nothing obvious. What about the floor?"

Ayuni crouched. "Nothing likely."

Muka was peering at the writing, tracing each word with his hand, pushing against them but nothing changed. On the top step, Never sat and tapped his fingers on his knee. It didn't seem that any Amouni trick would be enough, but he could always try some blood, just in case.

"Look," Ayuni cried.

Never twisted. A soft yellow glow was spreading across the stone, starting from the point where Muka's lantern sat near.

"It's heat," Ayuni said. She removed the lantern and after a moment, the glow began to fade. "See?"

"Let's try something hotter then," Never said with a grin. "Would you like to try some fire?"

Ayuni cupped her hands and closed her eyes, mouth moving soundlessly, a slight furrow in her brow. Light flickered, flashes of blue and green – just like during the caravan attack. He took a step back, as did Muka. The light grew, heat pouring forth with it as Ayuni lifted her arms and placed her hands upon the door.

The fire swirled in place but swiftly the doors responded, turning yellow, orange and finally a searing white. Never gave more ground against the heat, until he and Muka were half a dozen steps back down the stair.

"Ayuni?" he called, shielding his eyes.

"I'm not hurt," she replied. A grinding followed her words and the light dimmed, heat eased. Never squinted up at the still-blazing doors, where her silhouette stood, shoulders heaving.

He joined her, Muka at his side.

Tears stood in Ayuni's eyes and her hand was free of flame when she pointed. "I can hardly see it."

Light was fading beyond the door, a wide stone cavern open to the elements, and beyond it rested a domed shape of polished stone, one side bright with the pink of a setting sun. Even as he stared, the light continued to slide from the surface, dwindling.

The shape was a mighty egg of stone. It stood larger than any inn where it rose above an overgrown garden, the sides smooth, gleaming.

"This can only be one place," Muka said reverently. "Home of the Great Phoenix."

"Truly?" Never asked.

He spread his hands. "I believe so, but we will soon find out."

Never took Ayuni's hand. "Should I lead you?"

"Thank you, but no." She blinked away the tears. "My vision has returned. I must see, quickly."

Ayuni started forward and Never followed close behind. Something was becoming clear – something he should have realised well before this point, yet he held off asking Ayuni about it a little longer. If he was correct, it seemed better for her to come to the same conclusion herself – if she hadn't already.

Muka touched Never's arm, lowering his voice. "Do you think she has realised?"

"No, but I think we should let her figure it out on her own."

The warrior nodded. "We will watch her."

Ayuni was already passing through the garden's fringe. Paved paths were being swallowed by grass and moss, near to purple in the evening shadows that fell courtesy of the giant stone egg. Bamboo sprang up from between stone fences and pale white benches arranged in circles, the litter from old leaves crunching underfoot. The trickle of water came too, from somewhere behind the egg.

She had reached the base now, one hand resting against it. A warm glow of orange spread from beneath her fingers, spiralling until each tendril hit an invisible barrier in the shape of a doorway. The entire slab was soon criss-crossed with light – at which point stone began to slide open.

The light faded, revealing a darkened entryway.

Ayuni strode forward without hesitation.

"Ayuni, wait." Never drew his knives as he followed, Muka pulling his sword free as they passed into darkness. But the passage was not long, and a glow waited beyond, warm light smouldering within stone walls of a vast chamber.

The room was lined with low stone benches, all facing a mighty nest. Crafted of black marble, it was the work of a master artisan. Every detail seemed as though it had but-recently been completed. The bend and gnarl of each twig, the textured pattern of bark visible on larger branches or the solid base of mud and dried grass was intricate; a few pieces seemed to hang free from the tangle, so real it seemed.

Only its gleam and colour gave it away as marble.

Ayuni sat in the row of seats nearest the nest, head in her hands. She looked up, tears in her eyes, when Never reached her. "I remember now... Mother and the other women, the feathers in their hair... I remember carrying my own tiny pail on the way back from the river, trying to help." She swallowed. "There are small homes of stone behind the Shrine..."

He sat beside her, taking one of her hands. "You have succeeded, Ayuni."

She smiled but drew a shuddering breath. "Have I? Never, I fear I know now exactly what I am – who I was destined to become – but I do not know if I can accept it."

"You speak of the Great Phoenix," Muka said, his voice soft.

She looked to the nest. "Within lies generations of ashes. Cold coals and the memory of fire, of songs of pure joy and chants of determination. It's all there, my past and my future

– my birthright. But it is cold and empty, what did Mother want me to do? Why did she leave me? I believed with all of my heart that when we finally found this place I would see her again. Am I a fool to have thought it possible?"

Footfalls echoed in the passage. "You are hardly a fool."

Brother Hiruso entered the light, carrying no weapon.

As before, he moved like a young man, taut with a hidden strength that lurked beneath silver and grey robes. His long hair, no longer white but now an inky black, hung beyond his shoulders, woven with dozens of silver beads. His face was barely lined now; he was a man in his prime – and all of it on the price of Ayuni's blood.

Flanking him were three warriors – the Hammers.

One Hammer wore a headband marked with Kiymako runes, he carried a bow. Another held a spear with a curved blade and the final man wore a *sisan* and carried a shorter sword in one hand. All bore impassively calm expressions.

"You will have to come through us," Never said as he stepped in front of Ayuni.

Muka joined him, the man was already breathing deep and evenly. Preparing his *lunai*? Never kept his attention on Hiruso. The fellow did not seem perturbed – why would he after their last encounter – but rather, quite pleased by his wide smile.

"Oh, I do hope it will not be so, Never."

"I will die before I let you take her, you know that."

He laughed. "Perhaps. But I don't think that will be necessary. For the Great Phoenix clearly favours me."

"That's comforting to know."

"Isn't it? Ah, Never. You cannot understand how gratifying it is to have so many pieces fall into place at once, with so little effort on my part – especially considering how long I have wanted to enter this Shrine, but fortunately you and your sister were considerate enough to lead us here and Ayuni herself kind enough to open the way."

"I did no such thing!" Ayuni charged forward with a shout but Never caught her arm. His own jaw was clenched – no wonder the bastard had not pursued them too closely, no wonder escaping from Yalinamo went so smoothly. Hiruso *wanted* them to succeed; he needed them to uncover and then unseal the Shrine of the Great Phoenix.

"You certainly did, my dear. Seventeen long years I waited for your Awakening, but you have performed even better than I'd hoped. I owe this moment to you – no-one else could have opened the egg, only the daughter of the Phoenix herself."

"No." Ayuni gave a shiver and her eyes hardened. "You are not welcome here, usurper."

"That will soon be a moot point." He started forward slowly. "I do not wish to waste *your* blood if I can help it. So I will offer you surrender but once; I will give you the chance to spare the Amouni and the Sword of Stone, only once, Ayuni. Choose now."

"Do not believe him, Ayuni," Muka said, voice firm.

"Hiruso, you are wrong. I am a fool," Ayuni said. "But I have eyes. I see into your shrivelled heart. Begone lest I sear your flesh from your very bones."

Brother Hiruso snapped his fingers. "She must live."

The Hammers sprang forth.

Chapter 35

A bowstring snapped.

Never pulled Ayuni back as pain erupted in his leg. A shaft protruded, and blood poured down his thigh. Muka had already leapt forward to engage the spearman. Both fighters moved with the aid of their *lunai*, almost too fast to trace. Sparks flew when their weapons met, and they fought in and amongst the benches as if they faced off on level ground.

The Hammer with the tyrant was swooping in from the side, Never had already lost sight of the bowman when the bowstring twanged again.

A green burst of fire roared.

Something metallic hit the stones at his feet. Ayuni had burnt away the arrow's shaft! He only had a moment to release it, forced to leap forward and meet the swordsman. Never flung a dagger as he did, but the man dodged easily. Never had already drawn another, crossing the blades to catch the whistling sword.

The blow drove him back and before he could react, the

Hammer had swung his second blade, arm bearing its odd after-image, steel tearing into Never's side. Pain jolted him and Never spat a curse as the Hammer pushed him to the stone, heading for Ayuni. From his knees, Never let his wings burst free and beat them in a mighty blast, throwing the Hammer off balance just as Ayuni flung a wave of blue and green flames at the man.

It wasn't much but it was enough.

The scent of seared flesh filled the space between them.

A burnt husk fell to the floor, melted steel pooling on the stone.

Another arrow snapped and Ayuni cried out, clutching her calf. She hit the ground but flung another blast of flame, yet she was too slow – the Hammer was already moving in, bow forgotten, some manner of vial and cloth in his hands.

Never called the crimson-fire around him.

There was no way he could strike the archer directly. The Hammer would dodge any such attempt and more, the man was already upon Ayuni, cloth moving toward her face.

"No!" Never roared.

Burning blood exploded from his body. It tore through the air in all directions, there was no way to avoid it, and it covered Ayuni and the archer. Both were thrown back, falling in a heap. Never clawed his way to his feet, tearing the wound in his side further as he did, breath escaping in ragged gasps.

A figure stirred – Ayuni.

She stood, shaking her head as if groggy, but she was unharmed. Never shuddered with the relief; his gamble had paid off. No daughter of the Phoenix – doubtless with or without Amouni blood – was ever going to be harmed by the crimson-fire. The Hammer on the other hand was a sooty lump, unrecognisable.

Applause echoed in the Temple.

Never turned, using his wings to aid him since his injured leg was slow to respond. His body was afire with agony but at the same time, he was dimly aware of it working to heal, struggling against the onslaught of agony from his wounds.

But it was the man clapping his hands that held Never's gaze.

Brother Hiruso had not moved. "Look at what such a small victory has cost you." He gestured to Never and then off to the side, where Muka stood leaning on his tyrant, bleeding from half a dozen wounds. "Impressed as I am that you managed to defeat my best men, I will not accept further resistance now. Your blood has given me much, Ayuni but I will not be beholden to it forever. There is something I need from the Great Phoenix – and so I ask that you accompany me to the nest where you will call your Mother."

She shook her head. "I will not."

"I do doubt that." The monk lurched forward, appearing before Never in a flash. Hiruso held one of Never's own knives to his throat. "Final opportunity, girl."

Ayuni gaped.

"Burn us both," Never whispered to his sister.

Hiruso flinched.

A bloody sword point protruded from his chest. The monk glared at it as he fell back, spinning to backhand his attacker.

Muka flew across the chamber to crash to the ground, tumbling into the benches with a groan.

Pain and triumph warred across Hiruso's features. He

reached behind his back and jerked the blade free, letting it clatter to the stones. Blood ran down his robe, but it soon slowed to a trickle. "My my, how rich your blood, Ayuni. But it is a mere trinket to what I will soon possess."

"You do not understand what you seek," Ayuni said, her voice breaking.

"So young to preach," he replied. "Now, let us try again. Call your Mother if you wish for Never to survive."

Ayuni glanced to Never, then Muka and back to Never before her shoulders slumped. "You will spare them?"

"Ayuni, you cannot trust him," Never shouted, even as his legs began to buckle.

She smiled down at him. "Never, let me do this for you. Let me protect you, now."

Tears blurred his vision. "Ayuni!"

She looked back to Hiruso, lifting an arm to point at him. "Say it."

"I will spare them."

Ayuni closed her eyes. "Follow me now." She started toward the huge nest of marble, moving around and out of sight, Hiruso close behind, his blood-stained back the last thing Never saw before collapsing.

But he held onto consciousness.

When he looked up once more, both were gone. He clawed his way after them, hauling himself across the floor. After a time, Hiruso's voice rose in anger. Never growled as he dragged himself further, his limbs flagging. Even his wings were useless – he didn't have the strength to rise anyway and darkness was sweeping in.

Large, golden eyes appeared before him.

"Hin?"

The fae crept closer, again moving soundlessly on all fours – only now it was so much bigger than before, like a mastiff made of leaves and shoots. It tilted its head in its questioning way, and reached out a hand, plant-like fingers twitching.

"Sorry... I... have... nothing," he murmured.

But the *hin* did not turn away, instead, it hopped closer. Its hand wrapped around Never's wrist and he pulled back – or tried to – but his efforts were useless. The sucker-like fingers found a wound.

Warmth rushed through him.

He gasped. New energy flowed into his body, pulsing as it filled him. Pain receded and the dimness to his vision too; he was able to move once more. As the power faded, Never blinked. The *hin* was now as he'd first seen it, little more than a butterfly – two green leaves with yellow dots beating in place as it watched him stand. "Thank you," he said.

The *hin* bobbed, then faded away.

Never started around the black marble, his limbs responding slowly. It was enough, and by the time he reached the stair he was able to bound up them.

At the top, he froze.

Down in the centre of the nest, standing waist-deep in swirling ashes of black and grey, two figures were locked together. Ayuni blazed with blue and green fire, her features and form still clear where she clung to Hiruso. The monk was struggling to free himself, his face a rictus of fear and pain, his robes gone, seared away.

Clever girl!

Ayuni had played the man wonderfully – drawing him away from Never and Muka and into a place where she could destroy him.

Yet thus far, Brother Hiruso was resisting the flames.

As Never watched, parts of the monk's face, his arms and torso would sear and blacken, only to restore themselves as quickly as the flames burnt his flesh away. Ayuni flared brighter and Hiruso cursed but could not free himself. Yet still he resisted. Her fire grew brighter and hotter still – Never crouched, shielding himself from the intensity, even as she cried out, the flame wavering now.

Hiruso tore an arm free from her grip with a laugh.

"I don't think so," Never growled. He sliced into his palms and called the crimson-fire. The globes snapped up around his hands. He flung both arms down. Searing blood shot forth, striking the monk in the chest.

Hiruso howled.

Ayuni's flame brightened.

Never kept the stream blasting forth and Ayuni's own flames roared anew, drowning out Hiruso's shriek as his body shrivelled. Never began to pant, but he kept up the crimson-fire a little longer, until every scrap of blackened flesh slipped from the monk's bones.

And then, as Ayuni gave a twist of her hands, snapping the mere skeleton she now held, Never slumped to his knees, cutting the flow.

"And now, we rest," he said, collapsing once more.

Chapter 36

When he woke the flame around Ayuni had dimmed, but it remained bright enough to light the entire chamber – the softer green and blue now responding in the very stone of the walls, as if the whole temple was welcoming her. The remains of Brother Hiruso were buried within the still gently swirling ashes of the nest and peace filled Ayuni's face as she smiled up at Never.

"Never, it's working," Ayuni said. "She's here."

"Your mother?"

Ayuni nodded. "We've had a chance to talk and I understand now. And I know you must be in pain, but she wants to thank you for bringing me here."

"It was all you, sis."

She smiled, then closed her eyes. "I'll be listening."

Never glanced around but nothing changed – and then his eyes widened. The flames were growing around Ayuni, twisting and surging up toward the roof, filling the entire nest – yet they did not burn him. The figure continued to transform, Ayuni still at ease where she stood at the bottom, becoming a bird of fire, great wings outstretched to brush the tips of the walls, mighty beak open in a soundless cry. Blazing eyes bore down on him, yet it was a fierce joy he sensed, not anger.

Never of the Amouni, Brother to my Ayuni. You are most welcome here.

"Divine One."

Perhaps now, but I was once a young woman like Ayuni, full of shock and wonder – perhaps that is part of what drew me to your father.

"An unhappy memory, I imagine."

For the most part. The bird's fiery feathers drew closer to her body. *But he left me a gift – one that, while he later stole – you have returned. You are everything your father was not, you are true Amouni.*

Never swallowed back sudden tears. "Thank you."

I know you must have questions, but I cannot answer them all, I must complete the rebirth before the window of opportunity closes. I only regret that Ayuni must take the mantle so soon.

"What do you mean?"

In order to defeat Brother Hiruso, she evoked the rebirth ceremony. It cannot be interrupted, for if that were to come to pass there would be no Great Phoenix ever again and more – as the living embodiment of the Goddess, she cannot leave this shrine until her own child takes up the burden.

Never stared at Ayuni's face, still a picture of calm. Did she know what she was giving up? Not just her freedom but truly, her entire life. So many possibilities were now closed to Ayuni. "That is hardly fair, Great One."

I agree, yet Kiymako needs our line, just as the whole of the lands need the Amouni. Without us, the world is diminished.

"I do not know if I agree about the Amouni."

Do not judge all on your father. The bird began to shrink, a steady lessening. *Ayuni is at peace with her decision, for her sake I hope you can be as well. Do not fear, many will return to this place and make it sing with life once more. Sister Sikoka. Biyo and others.*

"Biyo?"

I was able to send him to aid you – you met him in the corral.

The disappearing guard! How long before they arrived?

She will not be lonely.

"I hope so."

I will not fade completely for some time yet. Search the rooms beyond the Shrine and you will find a token of my gratitude.

Ayuni opened her eyes, the flame still surrounding her, only now it was much tighter around her body, like a second skin. Still, she moved freely as she drifted up to stand before him, climbing a stair of ashes.

"Never."

He could not stop a sigh, though he'd meant to conceal it from her; he should have been able to control his selfishness. "Are you sure about this?"

"I am – all my life I have served others, only now I can make a far greater difference, I can be part of changing the Temple. My only regret is that I cannot travel to see my brother's homeland. Will you return to visit me, Never?"

He reached out with his birch hand, passing through the flames to touch her cheek a moment. "You know I will."

"Good."

Never glanced to the ashes, unsure of what to say next. "Is that the end of Hiruso, then?"

"Yes." She shuddered. "If nothing else, his patience was impressive – to wait so long for us to lead him here."

"I have to wonder what role Father played in this."

"Mother believes he forged an arrangement with the Temple after my birth, doubtless he did not wish for me to follow in mother's footsteps, since it would spoil his plans for me to bear more Amouni children."

"I will search his journals," Never said. He met her eyes. "What will you do now?"

"Prepare for those I have called – Sister Sikoka is among them. She will bring others and hopefully specific information about what Hiruso was doing with my blood. We will start slowly; I still have much to learn."

He nodded. At least she would not be alone long. And she was doubtless safe, since she was now the Great Phoenix. He'd been a fool not to see it sooner – there had been enough signs, chief among them the differences with her crimson-fire. But smaller clues ought to have been enough too, the way the Guides had not addressed her as 'master' as though she were more Phoenix than Amouni perhaps...

"Will you help Muka?" she asked. "He will be conscious soon."

"Of course."

"Farewell, Never – and thank you." She started back down toward the centre of the marble nest. "I must finish the ceremony now, but please remember your promise," she said with a smile. "I need my brother."

"I will."

He waited until she stood once more in the centre, where the light began to return, a swift brightness that he flinched from. When it eased, she was gone.

"Ayuni..." Never turned and made his way back down to the temple floor, his steps heavier than before. A familiar emptiness took its place within him – threatened to drag him down, but he held it at bay, even as he knew it would return soon enough. Instead, he checked on Muka, shifting the man into a more comfortable position, finding his pulse before heading outside.

The shrine's glow lit his way. A narrow path of paved stone led behind the egg to a trio of stone huts, and beyond, in a tier that led down, were more homes. All empty, all bearing overgrown gardens, but he chose the nearest, passing through an empty doorway.

Inside, he found a single large room with an empty bed and a cold stove, but a necklace of a dusky orange fire-stone lay curled at the end of the bed. He lifted the item, pulling it over his head. The stones were lighter than they seemed, resting easily beneath his tunic, beside the fang.

Yet no sense of its purpose was revealed and so he left with a murmur of thanks.

Chapter 37

Muka's injuries ensured that their journey back down the tunnel, through the abandoned Vale of Light, and down the mountain and beyond the Beshano River was a slow one, but it was uneventful at least – thanks to the charm. It continued to shield them from all they encountered, be they farmers or the handful of monks which were climbing up toward what would no doubt be a fruitless search.

Even if they did discover the hatch beneath the debris Never had replaced, he doubted Ayuni would welcome them.

The thought drew a sigh.

"You've been doing that for days," Muka said. He leant on his makeshift crutch, wiping beads of sweat from his brow where he rested beneath the shade of a tree. While he moved much easier now, he was not fully healed by any stretch. Bandages were still visible beneath the rips and tears in his clothing. Never's own wounds were healing quickly, though he was not likely to pick a fight with any of the monks just yet.

"I know."

"She is safe, Never."

"True." He dumped his pack and removed a water flask, taking a long drink. "There is that at least."

"And I do not wish to add to your burden, but I suspect it is time for you and I to part ways too. There is much that must be done to continue the rebellion, even with Hiruso finished but before that there is something I must see to before I seek Wanatek."

Never paused. "Are you sure—"

Muka pointed with a grin. "None of that from you – I can look after myself now."

Never chuckled. The man was probably telling the truth about his recovery, considering his *lunai*, and Never *would* be able to travel quicker alone but that did not mean he sought yet another parting so soon. Watching over Muka during the journey so far had nearly been enough to keep the emptiness at bay. "I wouldn't dream of it. And your mysterious task?"

"I wish to see my daughter."

He lowered the flask. "Your daughter? Is she nearby?"

"Somewhat. Iri made the charm you wear."

"You kept that secret well," Never said. Though perhaps it explained why Muka had hung back before leaving that day. And considering his role in the rebellion, such secrecy was a prudent way to safeguard her true identity.

He nodded. "As much for her protection as anything else."

"Then thank her for me." He lifted the fang. "It is impressive magic."

Muka wore a proud smile. "And what of your path, then?"

Never glanced to their back trail, toward the river. Father's journals were waiting. It was something he had to do alone. "I have a task of my own to complete. If it takes longer than I expect, we may meet again soon."

"Then may the Phoenix watch over you, Never of the Amouni," he said. "Which I am sure she will."

"And you, Sword of Stone," Never replied. He repacked his flask and stretched his arms a moment before letting his wings free. Then he leapt into the air, climbing quickly and heading back toward the Beshano.

He flew swiftly and when he landed once more on the Bridge of Mist, he found he could not recall a single detail of his flight, least of all how long it had taken. But he raised his voice over the waterfall and soon a Guide was taking him beneath the river and to the tiled vestibule.

He dismissed the Amouni relic as he opened the silver door, approaching his father's journals at a stride. Surely now, after so long, he would discover the truth. He had to. After losing Ayuni to her role as Phoenix, the Gods owed him! Just this much, just a name, *his* name – please.

At the bench, Never pulled a stool close and sat. He lifted the leather and found the page where he'd stopped reading, eyes hungry for the ancient words.

And as Never read, shock, the first of many emotions, rushed through him:

Jenisa refuses to call our sons the names I have chosen for them, even when I visit. She says only 'my boys' or 'beloved' or something similar in Quisoan. While it irks me to no end, it does not matter in the grand scheme of things, I am patient. Once they are old enough, I will take them with me and they will know their true names, names they will surely grow into – there is such potential swirling within their blood. I cannot be sure, but from all my research in the island archive it seems twins are

exceedingly rare for Amouni, doubly so for those whose sires are
already Ascended.

But that is merely another grand omen, surely.

My sons, pale Tekysar and Tekavesa so dark, together we will
restore the Amouni race and the true order of the world.

Never hurled the journal into the wall. The spine cracked as it thumped against stone.

Tekysar and Tekavesa.

Amouni words…but hardly names. And hardly the choice of a loving Father: Tekysar, *'to ruin'* and Tekavesa meaning *'to rebuild'*. He slumped into the stool, simply staring at the page, at the mere words his father gave as names, words Mother refused to use.

"By all the gods."

Never closed his eyes.

Beneath the storm of resentment, of shock and fury, of fresh pain, a sliver of sadness ran strong. There was no way to share what he'd learnt with Snow – and it was clear now, his brother had not visited the chamber, else Snow would have revealed their names. "I am sorry, brother."

Half his life he'd searched for his true name. He'd chased clues and rumours and hints from mouldering legends, searched everywhere from rivers, caves and mountains to libraries and palaces and it ended here at last, in the hush of an empty Amouni ruin, ending in the marks of his father's own forceful hand.

Never gasped out half a shuddering sob – yet anger followed on the heels of his dismay, simmering swiftly to a boil. He stood and swept the remaining journals from the bench with a roar, sending them tumbling across the floor.

"What legacy is this, Father?" he shouted. His voice echoed in the emptiness. "Well? You Gods-forsaken coward!"

Snow was 'to ruin' and Never supposedly 'to rebuild'. Rebuild what? The world and humanity? It was the very same Amouni conceit that supposedly 'lesser' people had long feared. Terrible names! Empty names too – like a final slap from beyond the grave from a man who had spared nary a thought for his sons beyond what they could do for his monstrous obsession.

Breath rasped in Never's throat and he scrambled for the resolve he'd found at mother's grave, clinging to it now, fists clenched. It was a resolve he'd forged for himself on that day – and even in his fury he realised, nothing had changed today.

He was *not* Tekavesa and nor was that *ever* true.

Snow had given him the only name that meant anything, and to the Burning Graves Below with Father and his poor prophecy. "I am *Never*." It was name enough; it had served him nearly all his life, by Pacela, it would do for the rest.

Never exhaled heavily. Some of the knotted emotion slipped free with the breath. He folded his arms. "That is my name."

Epilogue

Darkness cloaked Najin where Never hung from the mansion's eaves, wings aiding his balance as he worked at the latch on the bamboo shutters. Upside down, the blood ran to his head, but he ignored the discomfort as he slid a thin piece of steel between the shutters, gently lifting the latch free.

Once it had raised from the catch he used his fingertips to pull the shutter open, slipping the steel up his sleeve then dropping down to a balcony railing. He hid his wings then climbed onto the sill, pausing to listen.

Only the faint sound of his breathing.

Good. All were sleeping, it seemed. He placed one foot within, then the rest of his body before closing but not locking the window. Then, he padded across the room by what little light slipped through the shutters, heading for Isansho Shika's morbid gallery.

He drew the dark curtain back slowly, the brass hoops giving a soft hiss as he did, then moved within. The light was far poorer here, but he found the glass cases and paused to prick his forefinger, calling a tiny amount of crimson-fire, the red glow enough to find the display which held Hanael's ring.

Then he paused. A few possibilities presented themselves, but he'd planned on the quietest, even though it would be clear he'd visited. But then, leaving a sign behind was not so bad as leaving a trail – something he *wasn't* meaning to do.

He moved his finger over the glass and it began to melt, a hole spreading quickly. While the edges were still dripping, he reached in and lifted the ruby ring free. He let the crimson-fire die.

Then he turned and started back across the gallery floor, ignoring the paintings, and closed the curtain behind him, slowly still, since rushing *out* of a place was the oldest mistake.

In the room with the unlocked shutters, he pushed them open gently, letting moonlight in – then paused at the creak of wood.

"Welcome back, Never."

He spun, knives in hand.

Isansho Shika stood behind him, arms folded. She still wore her hair shaved high and still carried twin blades... yet something about her appeared different. Was her jaw a little softer now, her eyes a little less cold? Or was it the moonlight playing tricks on him? For even as he peered closer, her features seemed to return to what he remembered.

"Lady Shika."

"I bear a message."

"If it's about your dungeon I believe I can guess," he said, blades still in hand. He could still escape easily enough but not without her raising the alarm, which would doubtless sour his plans for the harbour. Never stared a little harder at her. There *was* something amiss with her face, yet his mind – or his eyes – could not fathom it

"Wanatek wishes you a safe voyage – we have opened the harbour, in case you had not heard, please go with the Isansho's blessing." She raised a rectangular token, holding it out for him to take. "Captain Milagra has been kind enough to wait for you. You will find your possessions on board."

And then everything fell into place.

The Lady Shika before him was *not* the one he'd met after being captured. This particular woman was an imposter, doubtless planted in the mansion by Wanatek. The woman offering him safe passage from Kiymako was owner of the voice he'd overheard in Okana, crouched beneath her window.

Just where was the true Shika? Prisoner or corpse? The latter probably would be the safer choice.

He took the token. "You have my thanks, Lady."

She nodded.

"Would you pass on a message of my own?"

"Of course."

"Please let Wanatek know that the Great Phoenix would be most happy to meet with him and that once Muka is fully healed, I'm sure he'll help with the journey east."

Did her eyes widen ever so slightly? "I will."

Lady Shika turned from the window then and Never grinned as he hopped onto the sill and leapt into the night.

Hello! While you wait for Never's next adventure, *Specture* - you might enjoy my other epic fantasy series, which begins with *City of Masks*:

A noble daughter burdened by power she never sought.

Perched on an unforgiving coast, the city of Anaskar is under threat from enemies within. Its own royal family feuds over possession of sentient bone masks of power, leaving Sofia Falco, daughter to the city's Lord Protector, to foil a conspiracy designed to strip her father of both his title and powerful Greatmask.

A bitter mercenary accused of murder.

Yet when disaster strikes, Sofia is forced to flee the palace and into the city where she crosses paths with mercenary Notch. But Notch has his own problems - accused of murder, he must fight to clear his name, all the while hunted by the city's robed assassins, the very people who are now searching for Sofia...

Follow two unlikely heroes on an epic fantasy adventure where the struggle over bone masks of powert hreatens to tear their city - and kingdom - into shreds.

Visit www.ashleycapes.com to learn more!

Acknowledgements

Above all, I'd like to thank those of you who made the Phoenix of Kiymako Kickstarter campaign such a success - you are indeed quite awesome!

Joshua C. Chadd ~ Levid José de Jesús Montes Sánchez ~ Frank Martin ~ Willman Duffy ~ Dianne Ascroft ~ Liz the Lucky ~ Sarah Martherus ~ Doug Grumpy ~ Amy C. ~ Sean Klope ~ Abigail Schuyler Du Verger ~ Lee Dunning ~ Catherine Stewart ~ Rolfe Westwood ~ Duke Talon ~ Michael J. Sullivan ~ Paz ~ Therese Guerette ~ William C. Tracy ~ Tasha Turner ~ Troy Osgood ~ Robert Karalash ~ Larry Couch ~ Daryl Parat ~ Lea G. ~ Melissa Shumake ~ Charli M. ~ Jesper Pettersen ~ Vicki Krebs ~ Heather Hayden ~ John Idlor ~ Jonathan Harris ~ Roman Pauer ~ Rita Canto ~ Ron C. Nieto ~ Oliver James Milne ~ Hyrulemaster77 ~ BL Draper ~ Leron Culbreath ~ Sebastien Jobin ~ Thái Thiện ~ Mark Siegel ~ Bethani Harimon ~ Fermin Serena Hortas ~ Jörg Sonnenberger ~ Berke ~ Guta ~ 6gun Sally ~ Kenny Beecher ~ Stephanie N. Chang ~ Rhel ná DecVandé ~ Jon Repreza ~ Jeff Lewis ~ Rachel Deegan ~ Bob Griggs ~ Suzie Gies ~ Chris Webb ~ Jeff Spires ~ Laurie M Edwards ~ L Austin ~ Nicki ~ Stephen Ballentine ~ Antony Lee ~ Nikki Tran ~ Skywings14 ~ Michael Dietrich ~ Mighobbes ~ Margaret St.John ~ Peter Curd ~ GMarkC ~ I-Cheng Chen ~ Kelly G. Smith ~ Mike A. Weber ~ Andy S ~ Cristan Silan ~ Franny Jay ~ GUSTHEDOGMYDOG ~ Kyle Brackman ~ Aaron S. ~ Steve Arensberg ~ Pablo Fernandez ~ Richard

Bunting ~ Jan-Henrik Wilhelm ~ Brian Griffin ~ Adam Goldstein ~ Chandler "Nikai" Hubbard ~ Olna Jenn Smith ~ Darcy M ~ Greg Tausch ~ David Queen ~ Ginea Merrill ~ Mark G Broda ~ Ashley Niels ~ SwordFire ~ Erin Himrod ~ Alyssa Staten ~ James Skala, Jr. ~ CJ Jessop ~ Brandon Carter ~ André Laude ~ Mari L. Yates ~ Riz Z ~ Daniel Lind ~ Kayla Moen ~ Belle McQuattie ~ Monica Elida Forssell ~ Sylvia L. Foil ~ Chris Vinson ~ Jenni D Strand ~ Tony Muzi ~ Mitchell Hogan ~ David Lars Chamberlain ~ Jennifer L. Pierce ~ Pierce Erickson ~ Rebecca Pendleton ~ Trava Buono ~ Sara Lundell ~ Jonathan Johnson ~ MidCity Comics LLC ~ Cheryl Caldwell ~ Lady Deborah McNally ~ Alexander Feliciano ~ Eric Krul ~ Paul y cod asyn Jarman ~ FyreSeer ~ Andromeda Taylor ~ Mitchell McLeod

As ever, my deep appreciation to Lin Hsiang for the amazing cover and also Vivid Covers for bringing everything together with the title design. Thanks also to David Schembri Studios for always making sure the formatting is spot on in the ebooks and my editor Amanda at Phoenix Editing!

Finally, to my loved ones - thank you too!

Thanks for reading and keep an eye out for *Spectre* - due 2019.

Ashley

About Ashley

Ashley is a poet, novelist and teacher living in Australia. Aside from reading and writing, he loves volleyball, Studio Ghibli and *Magnum PI*, easily one of the greatest television shows ever made.

You can find him online at Twitter or www.ashleycapes. com. As if that's not enough, you can also sign up to his newsletter there for free books, competitions, giveaways and sneak peeks of forthcoming titles!

Also by Ashley Capes

Fiction
The Fairy Wren
A Whisper of Leaves
Crossings
Somnus and the March Hare

The Bone Mask Trilogy
1. City of Masks
2. The Lost Mask
3. Greatmask

Book of Never
1 - 6
7. Spectre (forthcoming)